D0896862

DUCK AND DIVE

By G B Ralph

DUCK AND DIVE
Rise and Shine – Book One

G B RALPH

ISBN 978-0-473-59069-7 (Paperback POD)
ISBN 978-0-473-59070-3 (Epub)
ISBN 978-0-473-59071-0 (Kindle)

A catalogue record for this book is available
from the National Library of New Zealand.

G B Ralph
www.gbralph.com

For Te Peeti,
who encouraged me to tell people I'd written this thing.

Chapter 1
What's the hurry?

'I'm gay.'

I'd never said it out loud before.

'I'm gay,' I said again, staring myself down in the bathroom mirror. It wasn't so hard, I could tell them. 'I'm—'

'All right, mate! Bloody hell,' someone said. 'You're gay – I get it. Just let me take a shit in peace.'

My eyes went wide with horror. I was sure I had the bathroom to myself – was there another stall around the corner?

'I'm sorry! Sorry, I'm leaving…' My heart hammered as I shot from the bathroom. I dropped onto a nearby bench outside, head in my hands, red with embarrassment.

Then I realised… I'd just come out to someone, hadn't I? It was to a complete stranger, someone who hadn't even seen me. Still, it was a start, right?

I leapt to my feet, a fresh wave of anxiety rushing through me. The hidden shitter could step outside at any second. He'd see my face. See me all hot and bothered and know I was the blithering idiot who'd been coming out to his reflection.

Thinking only of distancing myself from that awkward situation, I ran along the decking, rounding the corner of the building—

And slammed straight into something. I rebounded, arms swinging as I stumbled back, about to crash on my backside when two arms shot out to catch me.

'Whoa, what's the hurry?' the something said, holding me in place as I got my legs back under myself.

Once I could support my own weight, I stood up and stepped back. Looking up to take in this wall of muscle properly for the first time, I almost lost my footing all over again.

He was stunning.

Thick legs, well-defined chest, wide shoulders, and sculpted arms – that's the word they used, wasn't it? *Sculpted*. I'd never had cause to use it, and now one such arm rested on my side, as if I could collapse at any moment. His form was evident despite being covered by the navy blue, driving range uniform. Finally I'd worked my way up past his name badge – 'Gabriel' – to make eye contact. His eyes were a deep brown colour, his skin a warm, olive tone. And his face – gorgeous, angelic even, how fitting – was caught somewhere between amused and concerned. 'You OK?' he said, head tilted to one side, wavy black mop jostling with the movement.

I was still speechless and gawking like a dork when someone tried to shuffle past us. My mind was too scrambled to process he'd come from the same direction I had – the bathroom. Not until I clocked the subtle lift of an eyebrow as he walked past did I realise who he must be – the reason for my mad dash.

'I… uh… yes, thanks,' I said, returning my attention to the man in the navy blue polo – Gabriel – as the other guy passed. 'Yes, I'm fine.' Despite having regained control of my body, my mind was still a few steps behind. 'Sorry, I was… I was in a hurry to get back to the tee. My friends will be waiting for me.'

'By all means, don't let me hold you back,' he said, smiling as he stepped aside and lowered his arm. 'But please try not to bowl over anyone else today. I don't want you hurting yourself.'

'I won't, promise.' Was… Was he flirting with me? No, he's clearly straight, just doing his job. Keep it in your pants.

Not knowing what to say next, I made my best decision of the day. I kept my mouth shut, gave him a small smile and nod, then headed back to my friends at the tee.

***

Jared and Richard were there waiting. None of us were golfers, but at the driving range it didn't matter how you chopped it, each swing was a fresh chance. It was great for a laugh too. We even had a few kids with their mum and dad giving it a go at the tee next to us. Wholesome family fun.

'There he is! We thought you'd fallen in,' Jared said. He was the loveliest guy – though a bit of a goof, and forever recycling the same, limited set of jokes. He only ate pre-approved, pre-packaged meals, which consisted – as far as I could tell – solely of boiled chicken breast and steamed vegetables. I sometimes wondered if this strict regime prescribed by his personal trainer had impaired his brain development, or maybe just the ability to think for himself. His alcohol intake wouldn't help with this either, probably

9

rendered the diet pointless too.

And he was forever falling victim to girls who only wanted a beefcake on their arm. They'd trot him around town for a week or two then just call it off. He liked to pretend he was the player, but each time this happened it would break his soft, squishy little heart.

'Stop dicking around and get your arse over here. It's your shot.' That was Richard. He didn't have an inside voice, or any sense of decency. I'd never met anyone with such a filthy mouth – he could shoehorn an insult or curse into any sentence. And where Jared was beefy, Richard was just all cake – crumbs lost in his unkempt beard, or piling up on his paunch.

'Come on Arthur,' Jared said, cutting off Richard before he could voice any more choice phrases in front of the kids. 'Grab a club and get up there.'

Jared was my best friend, had been since primary school. We were inseparable – even now he still looked out for me. I felt bad keeping something so important from him, but was terrified coming out would impact our otherwise easy friendship. We still saw each other every week, often multiple times, despite not living so close anymore and both working full-time.

Stepping up to the tee, I took some practise swings, hoping to calm down. Relax and try to enjoy my weekend. I didn't have to tell them right now, maybe later.

On my third trial swing Richard leapt up. 'Arthur, what is wrong with you? You're wound tighter than a nun's c—'

A scandalised gasp from the next tee cut across Richard, parents clapping hands over the ears of their impressionable youngsters.

'Yeah, loosen up or you'll throw your back out, old boy,'

Jared said.

'You're so stiff, and not in a good way,' Richard said, grabbing me from behind. 'Just swing the hips.' Pressing himself into me, he gyrated my hips together with his, first side to side, then thrusting forwards and backwards. Richard was laughing and whooping all the while, despite my protests.

I certainly wasn't relaxed now. If anything I was wound tighter than before.

Just hit the bloody ball. Then they can busy themselves with their next shots. That might buy me a couple minutes to sort myself out.

Still, rigid with all the pressure and stress, I swung hard.

I knew before I'd even hit the ball that my stroke was off. As I connected with the golf ball, I felt a slight twinge in my lower back. On the upswing, my spine was set alight. Screaming in shock at the sudden and excruciating pain, I collapsed where I stood. My head hit the decking hard, and I blacked out.

Chapter 2
What's the treatment, doc?

I had a splitting headache. And what was I sleeping on… a footstool? My back was killing me. This would be a hangover for the books, I could feel it.

Determined to get up and not waste what remained of my day, I tentatively opened one eye.

Where I was expecting my bedroom ceiling – paint starting to peel in a few places, unmistakable – instead a face confronted me. A beautiful, tanned, light brown face, topped with waves of loose, black hair. And that face was frowning, creases between the eyebrows – concerned is what it was.

'There he is,' the face said, breaking into a smile like sunshine. 'Awake at last.' Who was this—

Did I bring a guy home? I wouldn't dare… Where had he gone now? What was—

'Artie-farts, we thought you were a goner.' Richard's hairy mug crowded into my vision, grinning like a goon.

What was happening? I made to get up when Jared appeared next to the other two. 'Whoa mate, you stay where you are for a minute,' he said, resting his hand on my chest.

'What… What happened?'

'You were so stiff you snapped your spine on the upswing,' Richard said, solemn. 'Then you collapsed and cracked your skull open. Doctor reckons you have an hour to live, maybe two.' His lip had twitched as he finished before bursting out laughing.

'Dickhead.' I looked to Jared who'd just stuck his head in – he wasn't such a smart arse, he'd give me a straight answer.

'You swung so hard you knocked yourself out,' Jared said in awe. 'Not your best shot either.'

I gritted my teeth and tried again with the mystery man. 'What. Happened. To. Me.'

'You might have pulled a muscle in your back. Then hit your head when you fell over, so perhaps a concussion too.'

I nodded. A sharp pain shot through my body and I gasped out loud.

'Try not to move,' the gorgeous man said – Gabriel, that's right, golf range employee – reappearing in my view. 'Try to relax. The paramedics are on their way.'

Seeing him was a pleasant distraction. And I was determined to do as he said this time, considering he'd told me not to injure myself only minutes earlier. He wasn't being serious about that though, was he? It's just something you say. And I'd been too busy swooning and trying to avoid making a tit of myself to register anything he was actually saying.

Well, if I hadn't embarrassed myself before, I had now.

I groaned.

Gabriel's gentle concern turned to alarm, 'They can't be far away! Hold on a bit longer.'

I started to protest that I wasn't groaning from the pain, sharp as it was. But then realised I couldn't explain what I was really making a fuss about.

As if the paramedics sensed I needed saving from my shame, there they were, looking capable in their uniforms and carrying all that equipment.

'It's getting crowded in here – you boys go down a few bays and keep playing,' Gabriel said – my hero. 'I'll keep an eye on Arthur here while the paramedics do their thing.'

Richard didn't need telling twice and Jared soon followed when I told him I was all right.

I admit, I was thankful they were gone. I was pleased to have Gabriel's attention – even if flat on my back – but had been uncomfortably aware of my friends. They'd been right in my face, making stupid comments.

The paramedics introduced themselves – Susan and Connor – then with Gabriel overseeing they poked and prodded, asking how this felt? And what about this?

Eventually they eased me up into a sitting position, then with the help of Gabriel, to standing.

They stood back – time for the verdict.

'Mr Fenwick, you've strained your back and got yourself a mild concussion,' Susan said. 'Some rest, ice packs, and painkillers is all you need. Take it easy, nothing fancy.' The paramedics started packing up their things as Jared and Richard returned to investigate.

'What's the treatment, doc?' Jared said.

'Do we need to put him down?' Richard added. 'Put the poor old boy out of his misery? Knock him on the head a bit harder. What have I got here… a 5-iron, will that do?'

'He'll live,' she said, not appreciating the flippant attitude. 'Mr Fenwick, you'll be back to normal in a few days. It's best to keep moving so you don't get stiff, but nothing too vigorous. Only a little to begin with, then slowly more, as much as you can without too much discomfort.'

'Don't worry, miss, we'll be gentle with him to start,' Richard said with a grin and a wink, 'then we'll work our way up to "vigorous".'

'Uh huh…' the paramedic said, pursing her lips as she turned from Richard back to me. 'Mr Fenwick, have you got someone at home' – she paused, looking again at Richard and Jared – 'someone responsible who can keep an eye out during your recovery?'

'No, no. I'll be fine – I live by myself and I can look after myself.'

'That's admirable Mr Fenwick, but in this situation, also irresponsible. You at least need someone to check in.'

'Don't worry, I'll keep an eye out for him,' Jared said. 'He can stay at mine – he spends half his time at my place anyway.'

'You're out of town for work, aren't you?' I said. 'Leaving early tomorrow?'

'Shit… Yeah, I am,' Jared said. He looked stricken for a moment, then resolute. 'I'll call the boss, tell him he'll have to put me on something local for the week – then I can keep tabs on our invalid.'

'Mate, you know you can't do that. I'll be fine, I could—'

'I can look after him.' That was Gabriel, my gorgeous driving range employee.

'What,' I said, eloquent as ever.

'I've only got a few shifts here, and I'm fairly light at uni this week,' Gabriel said. 'It'll be no trouble.'

'Excellent,' Susan said before I could protest, as if she'd settled the matter. 'Arthur, you shouldn't have any problems. But it's prudent to have someone around, or at least not far away, in case you pull your back again and injure yourself in the fall.'

Turning back to Gabriel, Susan started ticking off fingers, 'He's to have no alcohol.'

'Of course.'

'And avoid applying heat to the strain, so no heat packs or hot baths.'

At the mention of a hot bath, my immediate thought – naturally – was of the toned, uniformed man in front of me. Naked. Enjoying a bubble bath at home, sipping gin and tonics, with me. Then in a swift and jarring transition, my thoughts turned to him nursing me like an invalid. It was all very confusing, from dream fantasy to horror nightmare in a heartbeat. 'I don't… I don't tend to take baths,' I said. It was all I could come up with.

Richard gasped, scandalised, 'You filthy, stinky beast!'

'Jog on Richard.'

'Showers are fine,' Susan said, taking back control of the situation. 'Just remember, you won't have the flexibility of movement you're used to, so make sure someone is around in case you slip.'

My imagination was already running away with me when Richard gasped again. 'Miss, do we need to hire him a nurse, to help him scrub where his crippled body can't reach? A nice looking girl to distract him from his pain. Preferably one with huge ti—'

'Shut up Richard!'

He clamped his jaws together and bulged his eyes in mock protest.

'Richard is a waste of space who promises not to interrupt again,' I said to Susan. 'Sorry, please go on.'

'Thank you, Mr Fenwick. Last one: no massages, at least to begin with. Maybe after a few days you can try a gentle back rub. Just listen to your body and don't jump straight in with a deep tissue massage.'

Richard whimpered with restraint.

'All right, that's it. We're off,' Susan said. 'You boys behave yourselves.'

'Anything for you, Susan,' Richard said, unable to help himself.

'Really?' I said once the paramedics were out of earshot. It was better to focus on Richard's unnecessary commentary than risk thinking about Gabriel's hands on me, gentle or otherwise.

'What? I wasn't interrupting. Would've been rude to leave her farewell unacknowledged. I expect your mother – my dear Denise – would have taught young Arthur better manners than this,' he said, jabbing my chest for emphasis.

'Ow! Stop it.' I should have learnt by now that reasoning was pointless. Richard loved putting on a show – he could go all day, his justifications getting more elaborate and outlandish as the debate wore on. I wasn't in the right frame of mind to play along today. Not that he required input from others – he was quite capable on his own.

'Susan can hold her own, don't you worry. Didn't you hear her going on about boozy hot baths, sensual massages and all the rest? She wanted a piece of our Arthur, I'm telling you!'

Kill me. Apparently my earlier embarrassment was only a taster. All I wanted now was the deck to open up and swallow me whole, never to be seen again.

Richard was too busy having a great time – whooping and thrusting and grunting – to notice my extreme discomfort. Not that he cared or would change even if he did.

'Right, let's get out of here guys,' Jared said, heading off to the car. Richard was a bit much sometimes, and on occasion Jared could be uncharacteristically perceptive.

I followed, taking care with each step, but not in too much pain.

Gabriel darted around to cut me off, 'I'll stop by in the morning to make sure you're still alive.'

'Oh no, that's OK. You really don't have to, it's not your job. I only went along with it to appease Susan... I'll be fine.'

'That's what you said to me before, remember? Yet, here we are,' Gabriel said, smiling. He had a point. 'It would put my mind at ease to check in, considering you did yourself in on my watch.'

'But, I hardly know you,' I said.

'Nobody knows anyone, at least to begin with,' he said.

My fuzzy brain couldn't come up with any other reason he shouldn't check in on me. Jared and Richard knew he'd be coming, my witnesses – if I was done in by this stunning stranger, he would be the number one suspect. Him checking in was the prudent thing to do. And truth told, I was not averse to seeing him again, even in my current state.

'Come on Quasimodo!' Richard said, shouting across the carpark and slapping Jared's car roof in impatience. 'Stop jerking about over there, you bellend. Gotta go pack away all your grubby magazines before old mate Gabriel stops by.'

I gritted my teeth and gave Gabriel an apologetic look. We exchanged numbers and he took down my address.

'I'll be around in the morning – let me know if you need

anything picked up, all right?' he said. Gabriel was resting his hand on the side of my shoulder, making sure I was paying attention but careful not to add any weight.

'Oh no, nothing – you're already doing more than enough.'

'I'll bring breakfast then,' he said, treating me to that gorgeous smile again. 'Take it easy Arthur.'

I felt unexpectedly dejected when he removed his hand and turned to go back inside. Though watching his toned butt as he climbed the stairs went some way to lifting my spirits.

Chapter 3
What are you hiding from us?

'Time to pick up all my grubby magazines Richard,' I said as we arrived back at my place.

'Arthur, we both know you're too precious to leave any physical evidence lying around the house,' Richard said. 'I'll bet your laptop is full of filth though, dirty prick.'

'Then why did you yell it out across the bloody carpark?' I said, not acknowledging the rest of his comment.

'Calm your tits. I was just trying to hurry you up. We weren't hitting balls anymore so no point lingering at the range.'

I took the front steps with care – holding the handrail – and let us in as Richard blathered on. 'You'll have all day to natter with Nurse Gabriel tomorrow anyway. Pity Susan couldn't hook you up. A nice lady-nurse to give you the attention you need, a healing hand to release your pent-up tension,' he said, pumping the air as if he hadn't already made his meaning quite clear.

Maybe I should suggest I'd rather see what Gabriel's hands could do. That's one way to come out. Today's plan had been a spectacular fail. Not only was I as closeted as ever, but I had a beautiful straight man calling in tomorrow, and my flat was a mess. It was torture.

'All right, mate?' Jared said.

'What? Yep, yeah,' I said, only then realising I'd groaned out loud again. 'Just annoyed. Such a dumb injury.'

Looking around, I wondered when it was I'd last given this place a proper going over. I usually headed out to meet friends, Jared and Richard being the only ones who ever came over to mine, so I'd let standards slip at home. But now I was assessing the place with fresh eyes, conscious of what Gabriel would see. Laundry which had been airing on the rack for weeks. Letters and leaflets scattered across the bench. A haphazard stack of novels on the coffee table, along with numerous cups and glasses. Not the end of the world, but not the best first impression either.

'My flat is a tip,' I said. 'Do you guys mind helping tidy a bit?'

'Oh no you don't,' Richard said, shaking his head, amused. 'Just because you're in this pitiful state doesn't mean I'm going to run around like your mother. Plus, that would be insulting to your independence, wouldn't it?' He started clicking his fingers, deep in thought. 'I'm doing you a favour! If I picked up after you, how would you ever learn to keep your house in order?'

'You're throwing out anything that comes into your thick skull, aren't you?' Jared said.

'How about this... Arthur was happy enough with the state of his place this morning when he was fit and able – why not now? What are you hiding from us?' Richard said, asking the question that mattered.

'He's got you there buddy.'

'I'm just here to make sure you, my dear friend, are safely tucked up in bed—'

'It's not even six! I'm injured, not elderly. And I'm not going to bed yet,' I said.

'Well, in that case I might hang around for a bit – seeing as my time at the driving range was so rudely cut short,' Richard said, settling into the couch. 'Grab me a beer, will you Arthur? I've been here five minutes already and you haven't offered me any refreshment. Not only is cleanliness at an all-time low, but the hospitality is slipping around here too. Another item for me to raise with the lovely Denise when I see her next.'

I did as he asked, if only to shut him up for a minute. There was a slight twinge in my back as I pulled the fridge door open. I dropped the beer and bottle opener in Richard's lap – it wasn't worth the risk of bending over to place it on the table, or trying to pop the cap myself. 'Your refreshment, your highness.'

'Enough of that cheek old man.'

'I'm younger than you, Richard.'

'Yes, yes. But when you go throwing your back out hitting a little ball – badly I might add – that's something only old bastards do. You're 25 going on 65.'

'Speaking of – Arthur, your birthday's coming up soon, isn't it?' Jared said, dropping onto the couch with his own beer.

I'd really been hoping to breeze past my birthday this year. In recent years I'd organised some nice, low-key celebrations with a small bunch of friends. Pub lunch and a few pints. Comedy night. A trip to the go-cart track. Dinner and a show. You know, a good, chill night out.

But my mates prefer to go big. Once they knew what I was planning, they'd go and organise a follow-up which always got out of hand. I understand that I shouldn't be so ungrateful – I have friends willing to go the extra mile for me. But it starts to lose the shine when you've smashed your phone screen, lost your wallet and woken up in an airport coffee shop at the other end of the country with a barista tapping you on the shoulder.

Sometimes I just wished I could get away with something less extreme – it's *my* birthday.

'Nah, it's ages away,' I said. 'Anyway, dinner – should we order in? Thai?'

'Pizza!' Richard said.

'Chinese!' Jared said.

'Burgers!'

'Malaysian!'

'Fish and chips!'

After a heated debate that consisted chiefly of screaming different cuisines at each other, we compromised on Indian. It was no one's first choice tonight, but an acceptable runner-up for all.

Though, which takeaways won was irrelevant, because I'd won the argument – the primary purpose being to distract them from my upcoming birthday. Success.

Once we'd put in the order, we settled into our usual shit-talking and arguing over what to watch.

I tried to keep moving to avoid seizing up, like Susan had recommended. Fetching beers occasionally to placate the guys while I put dishes away, folded the piles of clean laundry, and stuffed unopened mail into a kitchen cupboard.

With my place looking less like a bombsite, I eased onto the couch next to Jared with my beer. Susan had said no alcohol, but I took that to mean not excessive alcohol. My body might go into shock if I went cold turkey, and that would be bad for my recovery. I couldn't take the risk.

Richard was laughing like a madman at the other end of the couch. Seinfeld, again. I've lost count how many times we've been subjected to this bloody show. It wasn't even that funny the first time – background noise at best.

'Arthur,' Jared said, as captivated by the TV as I was. 'I've been scrolling through my phone. Do you know what I was doing a year ago, today?'

I had a sneaking suspicion I knew exactly what, despite having spent the past twelve months trying to scrub it from my mind. My only option was to feign ignorance and hope I was wrong. 'Mm? No, what?'

'Videoing you. Up on stage. With a lovely pair of dancers,' Jared said, not bothering to mask his amusement.

'Hah! Yes, I volunteered our birthday boy,' Richard said. 'After that old geezer they'd had up there, the girls were well pleased to get their mitts onto our Arthur.'

'They were getting rather intimate, weren't they? Though, we need not rely on my patchy, drunken memory – not when we've got the footage right here,' Jared said, waving his phone around with a wild grin.

I shuddered, recalling the night with perfect, traumatic clarity.

'And funny you mention volunteering our dear friend… You're right, it was his birthday, wasn't it?' Jared said, as if the thought had only just occurred. 'Birthdays, famously an annual event for all.'

'Friday,' I said, not wanting to drag this out any longer.

'My birthday is on Friday.'

'Were you trying to sneak that past us?' Richard said in mock outrage. 'Scoundrel. That's – what? – five days from now? You haven't given us much time.'

That was the idea.

'Don't worry mate, we won't let this slide by uncelebrated,' Jared said.

Again, that is all I wanted.

'That's really not necessary, I'll organise something for us,' I said, ever hopeful.

'It's not about us, Arthur – it's about you on your big day,' Richard said.

'My big day? I'm not getting married.' I regretted saying that as soon as it fell out of my mouth.

'Obviously, we need to find you a girl first, and that's not going to happen kicking around the house, is it?' Richard said. 'Some sweet thing to rescue you from that passionate relationship you have with your right hand.'

'We'll sort it. You rest and recover,' Jared said, patting my knee in what I had to assume was an attempt at reassurance.

'We need you on top form by Friday. Can't have you meeting your future bride and blowing it because you couldn't perform,' Richard said, flashing his eyes wide.

'Can't have our dear friend leading the life of a spinster cat-lady before his thirtieth.'

'Perhaps I'd prefer the company of a houseful of cats?' I said. 'Probably cleaner and less irritating than you idiots.'

'Don't be daft,' Jared said. 'Now, we don't need to find your till-death-do-us-part woman. Let's not aim so high.' Turning to Richard he continued, 'You know, he hasn't had a girlfriend since secondary school, it's been years! Too picky I reckon.'

'Just because I'm not shacking up with a different girl every weekend, or lining up one "love of my life" after another, doesn't mean I'm too picky,' I said, my patience wearing thin.

'Whoa, buddy!' Richard said, putting his hands up in surrender. 'Put the claws away.'

'You understand we have your best interests at heart, right Arthur?'

I had to admit they did, even if they were jerks half the time.

'And as your friends we are duty-bound to look out for you. To help you celebrate your birthday.' Richard clicked his fingers and pointed at me, grinning ear to ear. 'I've decided what I'm getting you.'

'You really don't have to,' I said, which was my polite way of saying 'Not a bloody chance, I am terrified of anything that gets you that excited.'

'I insist. I think I have just what the doctor ordered, something to get some life back into that decrepit old body of yours.'

He's fishing, I know it. I don't respond.

'What is it?' Jared said, taking the bait.

'Well, what kind of friend would I be if I left you both in tortured suspense…'

He can't bloody help himself, I just know it'll be awful.

'I'm thinking – a birthday treat for our boy Arthur – a handsy lap dance from something nice and blonde to start. Then, maybe if things go well, I might even pitch in for the deluxe package – anything and everything up for grabs, literally.'

Yep, literally the worst thing he could have come up

26

with. But that was Richard: always enthusiastic, often misguided.

Though, I've only got myself to blame if I'm being honest. They're my mates – if I can't tell them I'm gay, who can I tell?

Now's as good a time as any to come out.

I've got to tell them…

I'm going to tell them.

Easing myself up on the couch, I'm careful not to ping my back again.

'Well, guys,' I said, trying to look my friends in the eye. 'About my birthday… I've actually uh… I've got something I've been meaning to tell you guys for a while now. I… Well, I—'

'Oh my god, girl. Spit it out already.'

Taking a deep breath, I resolve to do just that. 'Guys, I'm—'

Ding dong.

'Food's here!' Richard said, leaping from the couch. 'Thank fuck, I'm starving.'

Thank fuck indeed, I thought, pushing back into the couch. I wasn't really going to tell them, was I? I couldn't risk our friendship like that… No, I *would* tell them. Not telling them was doing my mates a disservice, they deserved to know.

While I played this back and forth in my head for the millionth time Jared fetched fresh beers from the fridge and Richard dropped the takeaways on the coffee table.

'OK!' Richard clapped his hands and rubbed them together in anticipation – this boy loves to eat. 'We've got the lamb rogan josh, chicken tikka masala, matar paneer, garlic naan, cheese naan, butter naan, biryani and some plain rice.' He announced each dish as he removed them from the takeaway bags, with Jared following behind piling up his plate.

'Art, you can fill us in on your yeast infection – or whatever it was – another time,' Richard said as he loaded up his own plate. 'I can't be hearing about that while I'm tucking into my curry.'

I wasn't about to correct him, because that would require providing an alternative explanation. Unlike before, I hadn't built up the head of steam I'd need to come out. Feeling as deflated as I did now didn't lend itself to big announcements.

Shuffling forwards on the couch, I lent over to pick up a plate for myself when Jared handed me the one he'd already loaded up. 'Can't have you reaching over and putting your old-man back out again.'

'Thanks man' I said, settling back into the couch, feeling guiltier than ever. These guys had my back, as I always knew they did. I just had to stop being so pathetic.

'Oof! White boy, your hole will be on fire after this,' Richard said, laughing as he swiped his naan through his curry. 'Ishaan has outdone himself – this curry is hot.'

'What? Which one?'

'All of them. They know how I like my curries down there – proper hot, not wussy white-man hot.'

'You know I can't eat this! I was raised on mashed potatoes and boiled veggies. Dad gets a sweat eating mild butter chicken. Mild! I'm not that bad, but you know "medium" is about the most my stomach can handle.'

'It's true,' Jared said, not bothering to mask his mirth. 'We went to Nando's once when we were kids. It was for Arthur's birthday even – how topical. His old man ordered his chicken with "Lemon and Herb" level spice... Knocked his socks off. He went bright red and fair chugged down the ice waters after that.'

'What even is "Lemon and Herb"?' Richard, of Pakistani heritage, asked around a mouthful of curry-soaked rice.

'It's the mildest level of spice they do. Dad thought he was being adventurous getting any spice at all, and not just having it plain.' I tore off a piece of butter naan, dipping the tip in the rogan josh. 'Those are the genes I'm working with here guys.'

That first bite set my taste buds alight, despite the tiny portion. So tasty. I know I'd enjoy this dinner if I got stuck in like I wanted to. But Richard was right, tomorrow it would utterly destroy me. And as unpleasant as that would be, of greater concern was the thought of me running for the toilet every two minutes while Gabriel was in the house.

'Don't worry mate, dig in. Just watch out you don't put your back out blasting yourself off the toilet seat later,' Richard said, laughing at his own joke.

'Exactly my point.'

'It's fine. Your guts will have recovered enough by Friday night,' Richard said, winking like a jackass. 'You know, in case your birthday treat gets carried away while she's down there and slips a digit—'

I jerk back in surprise, setting off a sharp pain in my back which rips a scream from me. Though once I realise I'm still in one piece and have my breathing under control, the stabbing feeling settles down to the customary dull ache. It was probably more the fright than actual damage that made me squeal.

I look about myself, seeing I've flipped my curry, naan and rice onto the rug, with the plate resting on top, as if to hide its shame.

Probably for the best… Better on the floor than wreaking havoc in my guts. Will be a bitch to clean though.

Looking up from the mess I'd made, Jared and Richard were staring at me, eyes wider than my overturned dinner plate.

Richard was the first to recover. 'All right, tight arse. I'll make sure she stays away from back there. You don't know what you're missing out on though, man.'

I admit, it was a genuine effort not to react to that one. Though, probably best for my health – physical and mental – if I don't respond or enquire.

'What was that about, mate?' Jared said, his initial shock giving way to concern. 'You all right?'

'Yeah, fine,' I said, trying to wave away the attention. 'Twigged my back and lost my dinner.'

'We can bloody well see that. What a drama! And such a waste too,' Richard said, shaking his head like a disappointed school teacher. 'It will devastate Ishaan when I tell him. All that hard work – on the floor!'

'Look who's making a scene now,' I said as I lifted myself off the couch, wary of doing myself an injury again.

I scooped my dinner from the floor with a dustpan, then attempted to remove the stain with carpet cleaner. I was hopeful the stain would magically vanish, like they do on TV. No such luck. It was only partially successful, with a faint orange-brown blob of discolouration left behind, though the busy pattern went some way to disguising the stain.

Meanwhile, my two fully ambulant friends were lounging on the couch, happily chowing down. To be fair, Jared had offered to help. But I preferred to keep myself busy and minimise the chance of conversation which had thus far this evening not been going my way. Richard hadn't offered to help, instead returned to his Seinfeld, grumbling whenever I blocked his view, like he didn't already know the show word for word. That's fine, as long as he wasn't focused on me.

But what was I going to have for dinner now? I stared into the fridge, willing something edible to appear. I had a random assortment of beer, cider, fizzy wine and half a bottle of gin. A few bottles of sauce, jars of jam, a tub of spreadable butter and a bottle of milk in the door. My last chance was the veggie drawers which produced one wisened old carrot, and half a head of soggy, slimy lettuce.

In summary: nothing.

As apprehensive as I am about having Gabriel here tomorrow, I'm beginning to appreciate some of the advantages. One, obviously, was getting to see him again. Another being the breakfast he'd promised, more crucial now than ever. With a sparsely stocked fridge and pantry though, I'll still have to make a trip out for food tomorrow.

While collecting the ingredients for my humble pieces of toast, I really began to acknowledge my sudden lack of flexibility. I'd never given it a second thought, just being able to grab things off the shelf, or out of the cupboard. Simple tasks. Now, each manoeuvre had to be calculated to minimise movement and the risk of overreaching.

Toast for dinner felt like cheating, but these were desperate times. I lathered on the butter while the toasted wholegrain was still hot, watching as it melted, soaking through the bread. Then a thin spread of Marmite on one piece – my savoury main course – and thick coating of raspberry jam on the other – dessert. If I counted my curry-dipped corner of naan as my starter, tonight was a three-course meal. Lavish.

I ate my toast in the kitchen, and by the time I'd tidied up again Jared and Richard were getting ready to head off.

'Probably wise you didn't eat this curry, mate,' Richard said, wiping his brow. 'Even I'm feeling the heat. You, my dear white boy, would have suffered some serious ring burn tomorrow.'

'Good thing I flipped it onto the mat then, hey?'

'Still a shame, but yes, for the best. I reckon you'd have stuffed your back reaching to wipe every five minutes. Nurse Gabriel will be here though, he can lend a helping hand.'

'Gross.' That was the last thing I wanted Gabriel doing back there.

'Hey, I tried to line you up with a nice girl,' Richard said, 'not my fault you ended up with sporty, nerd boy.'

'Don't write the old boy off just yet,' Jared said at the same time. 'I reckon he's got a solid ten years left in him yet.'

'Thanks mate,' I said, responding to Jared and pretending I didn't hear Richard. 'Just make sure you put me in one of them nice retirement homes, with the waterobics classes and bingo nights.'

'You love your weekly round of bingo with the old biddies, don't you?' Richard said.

'Well, you know—'

'I don't get it, Arthur, I really don't,' Jared said, shaking his head with a smile as he pulled on his jacket. 'I mean, a few years older, sure, go for it. But a few decades?'

'I thought you losers were leaving?' I said, trying to shoo them from the house.

'You're a true man of mystery,' Richard said, almost toppling over as he bent down to pull on his trainers. 'But you won't last long enough to join them in retirement if you don't learn to chill, man. You're like a giant rubber band ball of stress and secrecy, ready to ping at any moment.'

'Maybe the constant scrutiny of my non-existent sex life is what's setting me on edge?' I said, keeping it light. But I mean, it's not a lie.

'Don't be silly, you just don't know what's good for you,' Richard said, half out the door with Jared on the step behind him. 'Uncle Richard knows what you need. And what you need, my friend, is some sweet, sweet—'

'Out!' I slammed the door in his face.

Let's hope they don't read too much into that, just the usual banter. I'll have to tell them another time.

Chapter 4
Who's here this bloody early?

Ding dong.

What? Was that the door? I was having such a vivid dream. I was doing waterobics in the olympic swimming pool with the bingo ladies – something I've never done before. Our instructor seemed familiar, in that hazy dream-like way. He was standing at the side of the pool, running the class, and I couldn't take my eyes off his arms. I just knew the rest of him would be equally toned, despite the shapeless nurse's scrubs he was in. The wavy, black mop of hair on his head jostled as he demonstrated each exercise with the foam noodle between his legs. He moved from one position to the next, catching my eye during one transition, winking as he tugged his noodle. I was suddenly very aware of the foam noodle pressed between my own legs. I was—

Ding dong.

What? Damn, I'd dozed off. Who's here this bloody

early?

Rolling out of bed in a hurry I felt a sharp twinge in my back – how could I have forgotten?

I grabbed a pair of grey track pants from a pile on the dresser. I wasn't nude anymore, but these track pants were doing nothing to cover my body's reaction to that weird dream – was I swimming? Or at the hospital? I couldn't remember.

Knock knock knock.

'Shit.' I pulled a t-shirt from the floor over my head, easing my arms through with care, mindful of not making any sudden movements. Looking down, I realised I couldn't walk out as I was. I tucked it up under the elastic waistband and hoped for the best as I made my way to the front door.

I'm not expecting any deliveries, am I?

If this is Patty from next door again, I will lose it. She's forever turning up with unsolicited containers of spiced apple muffins.

I hate spiced apple muffins.

Who even does that these days? Why couldn't I have normal neighbours, ones you never actually met or talk to? You might acknowledge each other with a nod now and then if you're feeling community-spirited. No more than that.

I rubbed the sleep from my eyes, pulling open the front door.

There was a man standing on my step. Tanned olive skin, a head of wavy, black hair. Smiling, his lean muscled arms were laden with bags.

'Nurse Gabriel,' I said before I could stop myself, stumbling back in sleep-addled confusion. My back twitched as I grabbed the door frame for support, my waistband-restraint shifting with all the movement. I'd felt myself spring loose, and hurriedly bent forwards to mask the sudden tenting in my track pants.

'Arthur!' Gabriel dropped the shopping and leapt through the front door, stooping over to help me up.

'No! No, no. It's OK. Just surprised, twigged my back…' I said. 'I need to stay in this position for a minute until everything calms down.' Little did he know. 'I'll be fine, just hold back for a sec.'

Gabriel hovered awkwardly, feeling helpless but not wanting to make things worse.

'Sorry if I rushed you, I didn't mean to. I wasn't sure the doorbell was working.'

'Yeah, it works, I was asleep. Took me a minute to get myself together and get out here. I didn't know it was you, I would have, um… I, uh, hadn't expected you so early.'

'It's almost eleven… Sorry, I thought I said I'd come around in the morning.'

'You did, you did. Please stop apologising,' I said, returning myself to vertical. I don't know if it was the shock, the twitch of pain or the embarrassment… Whatever it was, I was confident I wouldn't be poking anyone's eye out any more. 'I must have needed the rest, I slept right through, sorry.'

'Now you're the one who shouldn't be apologising.' Gabriel must have been satisfied I wasn't about to knock myself out again so he went about gathering the groceries. It looked like he had four fully-loaded reusable supermarket bags. Two had split open – so much for being 'bags for life' – so he had to take a few trips carrying armfuls of groceries into the flat. He waved me down when I offered to help.

'Are you moving in?' I said, intending it as a joke but

immediately becoming self-conscious about it. What was it about this guy that got me all flustered?

'I didn't think to ask if you had any dietary requirements...' he said, looking serious. 'So, I came with options.'

'That's very thoughtful, but I can eat anything, really. I mean, there are some things I don't like – like extra fishy seafood, or olives, or peanut butter – but they're not going to kill me or anything. And I'm not vegetarian, or pescatarian, or flexitarian, lactose intolerant, or coeliac, or vegan, or anything like that. Oh, you're not one of those are you? I don't mean like "one of those" like it's a bad thing or anything, I just meant to ask, are you?' Shut up, shut up. Stop babbling.

He smiled before responding, 'No, I'm full omnivore, and nothing will make me explode.'

'Me too, or, me either. Except really spicy food – delicious, but that's a recipe for disaster.' Ew. Why did I say that? Why am I still talking? Shut up right now.

Gabriel laughed this time – had I heard him laugh before? It was a hearty laugh, full-bodied, no restraint.

It made me smile. Fuck me, I was falling for this straight boy – falling hard. And he was only here making pity deliveries, being a good citizen and all that.

'Anyway, as promised, I come bearing breakfast,' Gabriel said. 'And I picked up a few staples too. I thought you probably weren't fit to be making trips out of the house to get supplies, as you are in your current condition.'

'I'm not pregnant!' Not yet anyway... Stop that. Mind, out of the gutter, now.

Gabriel didn't respond. But then I caught the twitch of his lip as he turned and continued unpacking the intact bags onto the kitchen bench.

I spotted some takeaway coffee cups. 'Is that coffee I see? Proper coffee?'

'I didn't know how you took your coffee, or if you even drink coffee, so I got a selection,' he said, pulling out one cup after another. 'Your options are a regular latte, oat flat white, almond cappuccino, Americano, and a regular hot chocolate.'

'Wow. That's quite the selection, we're going to be bouncing off the walls.'

He laughed. 'The barista gave me a filthy look when I asked for all these with different milks.'

'To be honest, I would've been more than happy if you'd turned up with a cup of instant.'

'I didn't think to buy any,' Gabriel said, frowning at the oversight.

'Oh no, I don't need any, there's plenty in the cupboard. I—'

'Which cupboard? I'll make you one.'

'No, no, no. I just meant you didn't need to go to such effort and expense buying the coffee shop's entire menu,' I said, but he was already making a beeline for the cupboard above the kettle. Unfortunately, that was where I'd stuffed all my unopened letters and junk mail last night.

Flinging the cupboard open, Gabriel was left scrambling to catch the avalanche of mail as it poured out.

For the second time in as many days I wanted the floor to open up and swallow me whole.

'Sorry, I should've warned you,' I said as Gabriel collected the last of my letters, adding it to the stack. Not wanting the conversation to linger on my general untidiness I suggested I'd take the oat flat white, 'Which one are you having?'

He grabbed the regular latte. We stood with our hips resting against the edge of the bench facing each other.

Silence.

I took a sip.

He took a sip.

More silence.

'So—'

Ding dong.

'I'd better see who that is, be right back.' Saved by the bell!

Why am I getting so tongue-tied over some straight guy? This gorgeous, thoughtful, charming straight guy, who feels bad that I injured myself and wants to look after me…

Uh, I'm infatuated. What am I, twelve years old?

Letting him run a few errands on my behalf will be like salve for his misplaced guilt. In the next day or two he'll realise that he can't blame himself for my injury and he'll vanish from my life. I mean, it happened on his watch, but it was all my fault.

I opened the door.

'Hello Arthur, dear!'

'Oh, hi Patty.' *Fuck.*

It was Patty, at full volume. Of course it was. Who else would it be?

'I noticed you were still at home – and on a weekday! I said to Philip that maybe you weren't well, and that I'd better come over and make sure everything was OK. Are you unwell? Are you off work? You look rather dishevelled – I hope you don't mind me saying – certainly not your usual handsome self! Did I wake you? Your hair is a right bird's nest.'

My hand shot to my head. I hadn't so much as glanced at a mirror yet.

Patty is normally so complimentary – uncomfortably so in fact. For her to make such comments, I must look a wreck. Not that I'm trying to impress anyone or anything... Besides, even if I'd wanted to, I could never recover from the double indignities of running straight into someone and then minutes later knocking myself out in front of them.

So, we've already established my first impressions were a disaster. And now, considering my current state of dress, personal hygiene and housekeeping, my second impressions: also a disaster.

At least I didn't waste all morning preening myself for my gentleman caller who was never interested in me in the first place.

I returned my attention to the middle-aged woman on my front door step, wearing what she called her 'home uniform'. This ensemble comprised white trainers, navy capri pants, a long sleeve top, and that lavender polar fleece vest she was never seen without. I swear she stole the look from one of the Desperate Housewives years ago – probably Lynette – and she's never looked back.

I couldn't get a word in. There was no stopping Patty once she got going, but still I maintained my defensive position in the middle of the doorway.

'A splash of water on your face wouldn't go amiss either. Have you eaten? You must eat, my boy. Get your strength up. I worry about you sometimes, all by yourself, with no woman to look after you! Here, I've brought over some muffins – your favourites, just in case,' she said, holding up the container. 'I'll just go—'

That's when Patty made her move.

She feinted to the left and ducked to the right, brushing past me her vest raised my arm hairs with static electricity.

'—put these away for later.'

It was an amateur move, but I wasn't at my most agile so she got away with it.

'Arthur! You didn't mention you had company,' she said, as if I'd had a chance to say so, and like that wasn't the precise reason for her being here. 'And who is this handsome young man? Well, Arthur, aren't you going to introduce me?' She stood expectantly on one side of the kitchen, Gabriel on the other, looking rather bemused.

'Ah, yes. Sorry, this is my neighbour—'

'Patricia, my dear. Patricia Binfield. So very nice to meet you.'

Known by all in the neighbourhood as Patty, or Aunty Pat to the kids. She only trotted out the full 'Patricia' when she was trying to be fancy, or flirty. In this situation I very much suspected it was the latter.

'And as happy as I am to keep on calling you Handsome' – nailed it – 'what do you prefer to go by?'

She was already making her way over to him. Despite my limited agility I managed to intercept my predatory neighbour before she could get her mitts on him. I knew she'd be dying to plant a big, sloppy kiss on his cheek or embrace him in an uncomfortably long hug.

'This is Gabriel,' I said. 'He studies at the university, and works at the driving range.'

'Smart and sporty! My, my… Double threat. A real heartbreaker, I'm sure,' she said, her eyes lingering on Gabriel before noticing the groceries sprawled across the kitchen bench. 'And what's all this? Arthur, as I've already mentioned, you hardly seem in a state to have been out

41

grocery shopping this morning.'

'Ah, yes. Gabriel picked this up for me.'

'He did?' she said, turning from the bench, gazing past Gabriel before settling back on me. 'He must be a very close friend to go running around after you like this.'

'We, uh, we met yesterday,' I admitted.

'Yesterday? Goodness, you move fast.'

'That's part of the problem, actually. I ran into him – literally – at the driving range.'

'I felt some responsibility for Arthur injuring himself,' Gabriel said. 'Bringing him breakfast and some supplies was the least I could do while he recovers.'

'No, it was all my doing,' I said. 'I'm just glad it wasn't one of the kids I bowled into, would've knocked them down flat.'

'Instead you knocked into this hunk of spunk,' Patty said, reaching out to squeeze his bicep. First she storms in here uninvited, now she's physically harassing my guest – she had to go.

Gabriel, facial expressions part way between alarmed and amused, jolted forwards and scooped up the unclaimed takeaway cups. 'Can I interest you in a hot drink, Patricia? We have an almond cappuccino, Americano, and a regular hot chocolate. The oat flat white and regular latte have already been claimed I'm afraid.'

Good move Gabriel, offer her a *takeaway* coffee – hint hint Patty.

'You're a sweetheart, aren't you? I'll have the almond cappuccino, thank you dear,' she said, accepting the offered cup and settling herself onto a kitchen stool. 'But, why so many?'

'I didn't know what Arthur liked,' Gabriel said, 'so I got

a range.'

'So thoughtful!' Patty said. If she wasn't in love before, she was now. 'And so good looking. Mmm.'

Patty took a sip of her coffee, and with her jabber hole occupied, I took my chance. 'Patty, it was so nice of you to drop in and check on me, but as you can see, I'm doing just fine. How about you take the hot chocolate with you too? I'm sure Philip would enjoy it, while it's hot.'

'That's very generous of you, I will certainly do that. My dear Philip though, he takes his hot drinks lukewarm. His gums are very sensitive to changes in temperature, you see, so there's no need to hurry.'

Was she serious right now? How do I get rid of this woman? I should know by now that Patty only leaves when Patty is good and ready to leave.

'Actually, Gabriel, while you're here I could use your opinion,' Patty said. I didn't like where this was going. 'Someone with a fresh set of eyes. You see, I've mentioned my niece – Samantha, gorgeous girl – to Arthur here a few times.'

A few times? A few times! I've lost count how many times she's tried to set me up with this poor niece of hers. Patty just won't let it go. I'm sure Samantha's lovely, but I refuse to play along because I'm not interested, and that's not fair on the girl.

I couldn't help but grimace. Gabriel noticed. Oops.

'I think they would make the most beautiful couple. But Arthur is maybe a tad shy? He keeps batting away my offers, like he doesn't think he'd be suitable for her or something. Can you believe that?' Patty said, in apparent disbelief.

I know what you're thinking. Simple solution: tell her

I'm gay. That would be an efficient way to put a stop to her well-meaning harassment. But you can't mention anything to Patty – our resident gossipmonger – unless you're ready for the whole neighbourhood to know. And as we all know – or don't, for that matter – I'm not ready.

And knowing my luck Patty will have a single gay nephew squirrelled away somewhere too. Out of the frying pan, into the fire.

'Now, Gabriel, you've only just met our Arthur, so I'm trusting you to be unbiased here, do you think you can do that for me? Put yourself in the shoes of a nice girl, like my niece, for example?'

He looked to me, somewhat baffled, before giving Patty a reluctant nod.

'Good, good. Yes. Now…' she said, walking over to me, one coffee-bearing hand raised and the other out towards me, like she was presenting Exhibit A. 'Disregarding his current unkempt state, would you say that our Arthur is a handsome man?'

'Right! OK Patty,' I said, taking her by the shoulders – gentle, yet firm – and guiding her away from Gabriel and out of the house. 'Gabriel has already been so kind in bringing me these coffees and groceries. I can't repay him by allowing you to ask such awkward, leading questions.'

'Pish posh, my dear boy. Now Gabriel, objectively speaking, Arthur is the type you could happily introduce to your folks, isn't he? But! Also – and I apologise in advance for being vulgar – he's someone you'd be more than happy to take back to your own place. I'm sure you know what I mean.'

Gabriel had been going to take a sip of his coffee but froze with the cup part way to his lips.

'That is definitely enough,' I said, making my second attempt to physically remove her from the premises. 'Gabriel is my guest, and some might consider this interrogation to be inhospitable.'

That's right, time for the big guns. Patty would rather die than be accused of acting inhospitably.

'I do know what you mean, Patty,' Gabriel said, the corner of his mouth quirking up as he spoke. 'And Arthur's already got me back to his place, hasn't he?'

What did he just say?

'Oh, you scoundrel! Such a wicked sense of humour.' Patty laughed. 'Now, that wasn't so hard, was it? And what did I tell you, Arthur? You've no need to be so coy. That settles it. I'll bring Samantha over next time she's visiting, and there'll be no more quibbling about it.'

Satisfied with her mission achieved, Patty pulled herself together while making the habitual breathy clucking noises that signalled her imminent departure. 'Well, I must let you go. Get well soon. And Arthur, my dear, make sure you call if you need anything, anything at all. That goes for you too, Gabriel. Ta-ra!' Then she turned – coffee and hot chocolate in each hand – and sailed out. As I shut the front door, I couldn't help catching her muttering to herself, 'Such a handsome young man.'

Chapter 5
What was he thinking?

I returned to the kitchen to find Gabriel smiling. 'So—'

'So that was Patty: resident gossip, scandal chaser, muffin baker, and unsolicited match-maker.'

'She seems… very involved.'

'Patty prides herself in knowing all the comings and goings – an A-grade curtain twitcher. There's no way she would not investigate you visiting.' I mean, I can hardly blame her wanting to get a closeup, just look at him. 'At least she always turns up with baking… I just wish I had the heart to tell her I'm deathly sick of spiced apple muffins. I complimented them once, now she's forever bringing them over.'

Gabriel had been in my kitchen the entire time, leaning against the bench, relaxed. He looked like a wholesome sport star having a domestic photoshoot for a women's lifestyle magazine. He tilted his head, smiling at my last comment. Mischievous, more indicative of a different type of magazine. 'Do you often have strange men coming to the house who Patty and her baking need to check in on?'

'What? Uh, no. No strange men – just the regulars. No, I don't mean that! I mean Jared and Richard, my friends – you met them yesterday.' I was well flustered and very conscious of it. What was he insinuating this supposed torrent of strange men were doing in my house? I could guess. Did he think... what was he thinking?

'I have to admit that I didn't much notice your friends yesterday. My attention was focussed elsewhere.'

Me. He was talking about me... Well, duh. I ran into him and then knocked myself out at his work while he was in charge, of course that focussed his attention on me.

I didn't know what to say, so talking about my friends seemed like a safe option. 'Jared and Richard are the only ones who stop in here. Patty knows them well enough now, probably too well. Despises Richard. "Uncouth" was the word she used, which I thought quite generous of her. He'd gotten sick of her showing up all the time, so one day he went all extra with the swearing and bawdy stories. Patty didn't think that was proper behaviour in front of a lady. She doesn't come over now if she sees Richard's truck out front.'

'He sounds fun, and just what you need to deal with your nosy neighbour.'

'True, I'm not really one for conflict though. Makes me uncomfortable...' Too serious, chill out man. 'Richard is fun though. A bit much sometimes, never a dull moment, that's for sure. His antics with Patty inspired me actually,' I said, laughing at the memory.

'Go on then,' Gabriel said, biting into a peach he'd unpacked from the groceries. You're killing me.

'Well,' I said, trying to focus my attention elsewhere, 'her youngest had recently moved out of home. I think Patty was feeling lost. She'd been using increasingly flimsy excuses to stop by for visits. I felt for her, kicking around in that big old house, just her and Philip. She wasn't used to it. But after the fifth visit in one week, I'd had enough. So... I fabricated a rumour I hoped would distract her for a bit. The place at number 43, just a few doors down, was up for sale. I mentioned to Patty I'd heard the mayor was considering making an offer on it. By the next day she'd whipped the neighbourhood into a frenzy. She had the entire street out in their front gardens pruning bushes, pulling weeds, water blasting paths, tidying away wheelie bins. She even had old Philip up a ladder touching up the paintwork on the front of the house. It kept her busy for at least a week. And as an added bonus the street had never looked better.'

Gabriel's smile had grown as I told my sordid tale. By the time I'd finished he was grinning ear to ear. My breath caught for a second as I realised all over again how stunning this man was. His face lit up my kitchen, banishing my earlier frustration with my uninvited guest.

'Well played, but it looks like your diversionary tactics have worn off. We might have to work on some fresh material. Make her think twice before stopping by so often... I have a few ideas.'

'Do tell, please.'

'How about I tell you next time I visit – does Wednesday work for you? I can't be stopping by two days in a row, I'd be in danger of becoming a pest like dear, well-meaning Patricia.'

'You could never!' Calm down, keep it cool. Mustn't seem too keen. 'Wednesday would be great, but you really don't have to.'

'No, I want to. Plus, our friend Susan would kill me if she knew I'd abandoned you after only one day.'

'She was quite fierce, wasn't she?'

'I dare not slack in providing your convalescent care. Speaking of, she would have my head if she thought I'd let you starve. Shall we eat?'

Judging by the ingredients arrayed on the bench, it looked like Gabriel had bought enough supplies for a few different, full on deluxe breakfasts. I said as much.

'It's like with the coffee,' Gabriel said, 'how could I know what you liked for breakfast?'

'You know, I would've been quite content with a cup of instant and bowl of cereal. It's what I'm used to during the week, before rushing out of the house.'

'Well, you're not rushing anywhere today, so a basic bowl of cereal won't cut it.'

'True. It's almost like a Saturday morning. I love taking my time on the weekend, trying something different for breakfast, or revisiting an old favourite. I'll eat anything and everything though – I'm easy.'

After a pause Gabriel said with a teasing smile, 'Is that so? Good to know.'

Oh, come on…

One suggestive comment I could pass off as general, light banter. But I'm seeing a pattern here – I'm not making this up, right? Either this guy suspects I'm gay, and the cocky bastard knows I'm hot on him so he's toying with me for his own entertainment. Prick. But why not, that's one way to amuse yourself while assuaging your misplaced guilt.

Or – and this is my eternally optimistic, gay little heart speaking – he's gay himself and dropping hints to see if I'll take the bait.

I'm still not ready to find out which it is. I don't think I could handle it if he was just messing with me for the fun of it. And if I don't demand confirmation either way, then I can go on fooling myself that it's the way I want.

Don't look in the box: Schrödinger's homo.

'So then, what's on the menu?' I said.

'Well, I've got a few options for us,' he said, checking over the groceries. 'Cream cheese bagels. Scrambled eggs on toast. Pancakes with banana, blueberries, bacon and maple syrup. Or a full English breakfast?'

My stomach was grumbling just thinking about all that food – my toast dinner was not cutting it. Though the slight stab of hunger I felt now was better than the burning, curry-fuelled alternative.

'I'm feeling pancakes. I haven't had them in forever, and I need something sweet.'

'Something sweet, coming up.'

He turned to clear space on the bench. And I couldn't stop staring as he rummaged around the cupboards and drawers looking for the big bowl and utensils.

He was gorgeous. And that butt – I was mesmerised.

After a few moments I saw he was grabbing the eggs, milk and flour and realised there was no pancake mix. 'You're making the pancakes… from scratch?'

'Sure, then we can have more if we want.'

Fair point. Looking more closely at the groceries I saw there were no ready meals or anything of the like. To be fair, pancakes are pretty basic, but all signs pointed to this man knowing his way around a kitchen…

Just marry me already.

Oops, my future husband was still talking – I'd tuned

out without realising.

'—grab a shower while I'm doing this? Susan mentioned you should have someone to hand in case you jarred your back and slipped. You might as well while I'm here.'

I hesitated. I mean, I definitely wanted to clean myself up. Can't have Gabriel thinking of me as an unwashed dirtbag. But I was quite content just watching his butt bop about as he made me breakfast.

'Unless you'd prefer I ask Patricia to come over and supervise?'

'You wouldn't dare.'

'I would,' he said, smiling. And I knew he meant it.

'Fine! Yes, I stink, I'm going.'

'The pancakes will be ready soon, so don't take too long. Or I'll assume you've knocked yourself out again – will have to come in and save you.'

I can't remember a time when I've been rendered speechless so many times in such quick succession. His 'threat' was almost enough to make me want to slip in the shower, just to see what would happen.

'Call out if you need anything,' Gabriel said.

What, like join me in the shower? Give me a hand scrubbing my back? The mere thought caused a stir. I was conscious again of the loose layer of fabric covering my bits in danger of becoming taut all over again. I turned in a hurry to hide the growing evidence and was rewarded with a short, sharp sting in my back – that was getting old real quick.

***

For better or worse – I couldn't decide which – my

showering went without incident. One slight twinge when I reached for the bodywash and face scrub, but no showstoppers.

I freshened up as fast as I dared. With teeth brushed, mouth rinsed, hair wrangled, armpits deodorised, and wearing a clean set of clothes – including underwear – I re-emerged.

'You scrub up all right,' Gabriel said as he peeled a banana. 'No disasters then? I don't need to call in Susan?'

'A couple of twinges, but I was careful. I'm hopeful I'll be back to normal in a couple days.'

'Good to hear,' Gabriel said with a smile. 'Now, while you were in there, I took a guess putting things away in the pantry, and tried to keep things within easy reach. Hope you don't mind.'

'Susan would be impressed.'

'I aim to please,' Gabriel said, holding up two plates of pancakes loaded with chopped banana, blueberries, bacon and swimming in maple syrup. 'And now I invite you to relax, and pull up a chair as the dining room proudly presents – your breakfast,' he said, laying down the plates with a flourish.

Was… was he paraphrasing Beauty and the Beast?

'Does that make you Lumière, then?'

Gabriel's eyes lit up, 'And you must be Belle.'

'Rude! Surely my role in this is the Beast? Unkempt and housebound, with loyal subjects to cook my meals and bring me muffins and coffee?'

'Valid points, all,' conceded Gabriel, smiling wider than ever.

'Though I must admit, I am a little disappointed.'

He frowned then, but said nothing.

'Where's my musical number?'

Gabriel laughed, 'Well, your furniture, crockery and cutlery just weren't up to the task. And I didn't have the time to teach them the routine.'

I couldn't keep up the act any more and started laughing myself as I sat down at the table. This guy was something else.

I snatched a glance at him as I took my first mouthful.

Delicious.

***

After Gabriel had left for his classes, I wandered about the house.

Entering my bedroom I moved some things around, dropped a few stray dirty socks in the washing basket, then left again.

I walked through the lounge, tapping my fingers along the back of the couch as I went. Peering out the window onto the street – what I imagine Patty spends much of her time at home doing – I saw a couple of cars drive past, nothing much else.

The fridge provided no distractions either. I stared for a minute before closing the door again.

Even my book didn't capture my attention. I put it down after reading the same paragraph three times and still not registering what it said.

Wednesday was so far away…

I checked my phone – no messages. Why would there be?

Should I message him? 'I'm going to message him.'

I drafted a message, then deleted it. I tried again,

agonising over the text, changing my mind countless times. Hey, or hi? Or just no greeting? Keep it general, or pick up a strand of our conversation from this morning? Emoji, or no emoji?

'What am I doing?' I said to my empty house. I deleted the text and slapped my phone face down on the bench in shame, glad no one had witnessed such embarrassingly adolescent behaviour.

I ended up binging TV all afternoon. Like an adult. Though after Netflix had asked if I was still watching for a second time I decided it was time to get off the couch and go to bed.

Chapter 6
How could she have known?

Tuesday morning I was up at a more respectable hour, showered, dressed and fed before I even thought to check my phone. It was still face down on the bench. Dead.

Well, that could have been a disaster. I should really be keeping it on me in case I stuff my back again.

I plugged it in and did some gentle stretching while I waited for it to come back to life. Easing into the stretches, I tested the muscles in my legs and butt and sides. Next up was some light abdominal exercises – my thinking being that if I could wake them up, they might help out in keeping my back in order.

After that brief round of stretches I was feeling a little more confident. Regaining the trust that my back wouldn't just ping at random – something I'd never given a second thought before. Is this what it's like for the elderly, but all the time, with no prospect of it ever going away? I bloody hope not. Maybe I can ask this evening?

My phone had a bit of juice now. I decided I'd update my boss, mention I was improving but would take tomorrow off to be sure. He was good about this kind of thing, would rather his team take the extra day off and make sure they didn't bring sickness into work and infect everyone else. Or in my case, didn't put my back out again by picking up a pen. The last thing my boss wanted was the health and safety manager drowning us both in paperwork.

A message popped up as my phone turned on.

It was from Gabriel, sent almost half an hour ago.

Did you survive your shower this morning, Belle?

'Hah!' My delight was quickly replaced with dread – what was I going to respond with? To save myself the anguish of yesterday I sent the first thing that came to mind.

Sorry, wrong number. This is the Beast.

Quite pleased with that, actually. I'd just sent this message when another came through.

Hey, if you haven't responded in ten minutes I'll have to assume you're in trouble and will come over. Let me know.

Oh shit, we must've both sent our messages at the same time. And he's been worried about me?

Sorry, my magic mirror was dead. Had to charge it up

Nailed it. It was only moments before a response came through.

No worries. Glad you're not dead. OK, class now, see you tomorrow.

As far as proclamations of love go, 'Glad you're not dead' isn't half bad. I decided to play it cool. His message didn't need a response, so I didn't respond.

Despite still not knowing if he was interested or not – or even if he was gay – I felt more settled about the situation. I was happy to see how this panned out.

***

I spent the afternoon lost in my book, and after an early dinner I was feeling up for my short walk down the road.

Tuesday was bingo night in the Activity Centre at Nana's retirement home – the Sunset Villas. I had been going with Mum and Dad since I was a kid. Nana always bought a strip of tickets and she would let me dab one for her sometimes. If I wasn't pressed up next to Nana, dabber in hand, then I'd be up the front helping Barry pull the numbers. Sometimes he'd even let me call them out.

One Tuesday Barry wasn't feeling well. He didn't want to dampen the mood in the hall with anything less than maximum enthusiasm – so he asked me to fill in.

I was terrified.

I was only in my mid-teens at the time – no one at school knew I came here every week, that would be social suicide. But here, surrounded by Nana and her friends, they didn't care if I made a fool of myself. This makeshift bingo hall was one place I felt at home, like I could just relax and have a bit of fun.

The old biddies – as Richard referred to them – were charmed with my bingo calling. Barry asked me to fill in more often as the years went by and his health deteriorated. I soon became their regular bingo caller, stopping by the retirement home after work.

Nana passed away just under two years ago now, but I'm still there most Tuesday nights. Nana's friends had become my friends and catching up with them each week helped me keep things in perspective.

I'd left myself plenty of time to get there and the staff were still setting up the tables when I arrived. They had an old-school ball cage with a turning handle – no modern, electronic random number generator for the residents of

Sunset Villas. Tonight wasn't about bringing in the big bucks, it was just a bit of fun.

'All right there, lad.' That was Gerry, a gruff old bastard to those who didn't know him. But to those who did, he was the biggest softy in this place.

'Hello sweetheart.' Gladys was another of my regular early arrivers. She was always here to secure her favourite spot well before the other punters. 'Is that a little twinkle I see in your eye? Have you finally gone and found yourself a nice, young lady then?'

How could she have known? I mean, she was off on one significant detail, but it's not like I'd ever corrected anyone, so could hardly blame her. She was one of my sharpest customers.

'I don't know,' I admitted. 'I don't think so… We'll see.' It was the truth.

'They would be silly not to lock you in, young man.'

'Thanks Gladys.'

Satisfied she'd dispensed her grandmotherly wisdom for the day, she settled into her spot, dabber at the ready.

Other residents were trickling in now, along with some of their friends who still lived at home but made the trip over for bingo night. Tuesday evening was a highlight on many a social calendar.

Here came Nora. She liked to think of herself as a 21-year-old woman stuck in the body of an 80-something year old lady. 'Arthur, my darling! You're looking even more handsome than usual.'

'He's only gone and met someone,' piped up Gladys. 'I think it might be serious.'

'Is that so?' Charles said, another regular who'd just sat himself down at the front. Charles sported the most alarmingly comical moustache you ever saw, Dr Eggman-style.

'If I'm to give you up to another,' Nora said, 'then you must bring them in so we can see what has set our Arthur's heart aflame.'

'Hear, hear,' Charles said.

'Oh I really don't—'

'What about next Tuesday?' Gladys said.

'My mystery love rival can help Arthur with his bingo balls,' Nora said.

This comment was met with equal parts amused tittering and harrumphs of disapproval.

'You get in there, boy!' That was Desmond, just pulling up a chair. He'd rediscovered his libido in later life and was wasting no time making full use of it. Desmond was a real character, though much of his humour is considered troublesome in modern times, leaning towards the sexist and inappropriate.

I was working on my rebuttal when the clock struck seven. Saved by the bell for the second time in two days.

'All right, folks. It's bingo time!' I said to the room, almost at capacity this evening. 'We have three prizes tonight. For our first game it looks like we have this lovely bottle of medium-dry sherry.' This was met with a round of appreciative nods and a serious few pulling their seats in a little closer. The Sunset Villas staff knew their audience.

'Next up we have a voucher which entitles the bearer to high tea for two at the garden centre cafe.' I noticed this caught Gladys' attention in particular.

'And finally, I have a note saying the winner will be given – subject to the approval of Brenda Myles, Sunset Villas Director – full control of the next group social outing.'

This announcement was met with gasps, a clamouring for dabbers, and even some spontaneous applause.

This was the big one. Brenda's social outing suggestion box was rammed with ideas from the residents, with very few ever being selected. Competition for this prize would be fierce.

I pulled the ball cage nice and close, minimising the amount I'd have to reach. The moment I started spinning I realised this probably wasn't the best thing to be doing with my stuffed back. But the stakes were high tonight, I couldn't let the residents down.

'As usual, our first game tonight will be Four Corners. OK folks, eyes down,' I said, pulling the first ball from the cage.

'17, dancing queen. 17.' Over the years I'd learnt the usual bingo lingo from Barry. Each and every number had its own rhyme or nickname. Sometimes he'd spice it up with some unique ones of his own – a tradition I liked to follow.

'51, I love my mum. 51,' I said. 'It's true.'

'11, legs 11.' The old boys responded with their best wolf whistles.

Another ball, '62, tickety boo. 62.'

'88, two fat ladies. 88.' That classic always got a cheer and a 'wobble, wobble' in response – tonight was no different.

'3, glass of sherry. 3.' This received an appreciative chuckle, considering the prize.

'69, your place or mine. 69.' For this I copped a few good-natured 'scoundrels' and a 'rascal' in response. Nora was wearing her cheekiest grin.

'84, sneak out the back door. 84.' Scandalised laughter erupted around the room, along with a 'cheeky little bastard' from Desmond – the cheekiest bastard of the lot. Nora grinned all the wider.

'42, the answer to the ultimate question of life, the universe, and everything. 42.' Charles enjoyed that one – he loved his science fiction classics.

'5, man alive—'

'Bingo!' It was none other than my not-so-secret admirer, Nora. She sprung from her seat and rushed forwards waving her winning ticket.

'I trust you, Nora. But I must be seen to be doing this properly or there'll be a riot. Especially after such a quick round,' I said in a conspiratorial whisper.

'Of course, of course.'

I checked over her ticket before announcing, 'Mrs Nora Appleby, you are indeed the winner of the fastest game of bingo I think I have ever called. Here's your prize,' I said, handing her the bottle of sherry.

'Thank you,' she said for all to hear. Then leaned in to whisper to only me, 'And you're welcome to join me in my room later for a celebratory glass if you like, dear.'

'Thank you Nora, perhaps another time.'

'You know where to find me if you change your mind.'

I did indeed. Nora had been slipping me her spare room key ever since I'd turned 21. I'd had to return it through her mail slot on countless occasions.

The second and third games went without incident. There was banter, I was ribbed by the oldies, all good fun.

Unfortunately Gladys wouldn't be taking home the high tea voucher she was so keen on. And for the grand prize – command of the next social outing – Brenda will be dismayed to hear that our resident rascal Desmond won that round. I dread to think what he'll come up with. It will be an unforgettable day for the residents, I'm sure.

The excitable clamour in the makeshift bingo hall faded as the residents shuffled off to their tea and biscuits in front of the late night news.

I was busy slotting the bingo balls back in the cage for the last time that evening and didn't see Gerry until he was right at my side. I noticed him just in time to brace for impact as he clapped me on the shoulder.

'You don't seem certain about this new sweetheart of yours,' he said.

Gerry's comment took me by surprise. I knew he was a big, old softy, but I'd never expected this.

'I just… I might be getting ahead of myself, is all. We've only seen each other twice.'

'That's all right lad, I knew from the moment I saw my Ava that she was the one for me. There's no logic in it, sometimes it just sneaks up on you and WHAM' – he slammed his big fist down on the caller's table – 'you're a mess of feelings and emotions and all that mushy stuff. There's no accounting for it.'

'Those were different times, Gerry.'

'They weren't that different, my boy. Not in these matters anyway,' he said, placing his hand on my shoulder – gently this time – and looking me directly in the eyes. 'You know your friends at Sunset Villas are here, if you need someone to talk to. Your nana would've been here if she could. But you'll have to make do with us.'

Then he nodded, turned and left the hall.

Chapter 7
Did this guy even hear himself?

I'm embarrassed to admit how much I thought about Gabriel yesterday. Like a schoolboy with a summer crush.

One benefit of being mostly housebound was that I was only embarrassing myself in front of myself. Then in public I thought I was doing all right keeping my thoughts and feelings to myself... But the eagle-eyed seniors had clocked me right away.

This morning I had exhausted my list of chores: showering, washing, tidying, dishes – all done.

I had reorganised the linen cupboard, and was now pulling everything out of my wardrobe, holding each item up in front of me one by one.

Did this spark joy? No? Gone!

My stretching routine this morning had been a vast improvement on the past couple of days. My body was feeling almost like itself again, and the physical activity was liberating.

But I was running out of things to keep me busy around the house. Earlier I'd tried again to settle into my book – something which had always come easy to me – not today.

Before Gabriel left on Monday, we'd locked in lunch for today. He had classes in the morning, and an evening shift at the driving range – late night – so said he'd stop by in between.

Of course I'd put up my token protest, 'Oh you really don't have to. It's too much.' But I was fooling no one.

It was still hours until Gabriel would turn up – I didn't even know exactly when. 'Lunch' time was infuriatingly vague. Was that noon? Half past? One o'clock? When my stomach started rumbling?

I was almost looking forward to being back at work tomorrow, if anything it'd be a distraction – might help me retain my sanity.

The doorbell rang while I dusted the ceiling light shades – who knew there was so much dust up there? I climbed down from the dining chair with care. My back had improved, not even a twinge this morning, but I wasn't going to tempt fate with any domestic parkour.

It was only a quarter past 11 – too early for lunch. And it wouldn't be Patty, Wednesday morning was when she met for Garden Club. Probably just someone trying to sell me beauty products, a new vacuum cleaner or enquiring if I'd heard the Good Word.

In my head I rehearsed my most polite, 'No, thank you, I'm not interested.' But when I opened the door, I found that I was interested, very much in fact.

'You're dressed!' he said. And the bastard had the cheek to sound surprised.

'Sorry to disappoint,' I said, indignant. Then feeling bold

I added, 'I can uh... I can go get undressed again, if you'd prefer?'

It was Gabriel's turn to be speechless, though he recovered quickly. 'Better not, you've gone to all the trouble,' he said, gesturing to me in my jeans and t-shirt, both freshly washed. 'And we can't be having lunch starkers – what would the neighbours think?'

'Patty would dine out on that for months.'

Gabriel smiled. 'Sorry for showing up so early,' he said, coming in with more armloads of bags. 'My second lecture was cancelled last minute – lecturer called in sick – so thought I'd come by.'

'No worries, I'm glad you did. I'm losing my mind here by myself.' That was true, he didn't need to know what I was losing my mind over.

'How's your back? You look like you're holding yourself well again, more comfortable.'

'Much better now.' Now that you're here.

No! Shut it. If Gabriel is half as perceptive as Gladys or Gerry, I'll be caught out again.

'I'm pleased.' Another smile – it seemed authentic too, not just relieved, like he didn't have to worry about an injury on his watch anymore, but genuinely pleased. 'I bought some more staples,' he said, dropping piles of groceries on the bench and starting to put them away. 'While I rummaged around the other day, I noticed you were low on a couple of things.'

'This really is too much food, again! You have to take it back.'

'Can't. I'm not going home till after my shift,' he said, then turned to face me. 'You'll just have to buy me lunch sometime instead.'

He'd only paused for a second, but it had felt pointed… Was he asking me out? Or, asking me to ask him out? Or just reminding me that I owed him?

'Ye – Yeah,' was all I could come up with. Lame.

'I thought I'd make a quiche today,' Gabriel said, mercifully moving the conversation along.

'A quiche?' I couldn't remember the last time I'd had quiche, not since mum had made one anyway.

'You mocking my baking? Not fashionable enough for you?'

'You sure you're not Patty in a Gabriel-suit?' I said, laughing. 'I love quiche. But it's a dish I would associate more with middle-aged ladies than… well, someone like you.'

'And what should someone like me be serving?' he said, hand on hip.

Yourself? I mean, fill me up.

Down, boy.

I had no legitimate response at the ready, so just said I was sure it would be delicious. 'Pastry, cheese, bacon, tomatoes, cream, eggs – it's what dreams are made of!'

I wasn't sure if my initial reaction had irked him or he was just winding me up. Regardless, his grin was back to maximum wattage, and I couldn't help but smile myself.

***

I 'supervised' while Gabriel prepared lunch. Really, I was just watching – could be the last chance I get. After today, he had no reason to stop by again. Even this visit wasn't necessary, but we'd already agreed on it, and I wasn't going to cancel.

Though, as he just said, I owed him a lunch. And maybe another meal to show my gratitude for him going above and beyond during my convalescence. Do I move it up to a dinner?

I owed him a breakfast too. If I'm doing this properly, I'd need to pay him back for that as well. He might as well just stay over between the dinner and the breakfast, save him travelling so much. Plus, it wouldn't be safe to drive after all those drinks I'd be serving with dinner.

Operation Beguile Gabriel was shaping up well.

'You know,' I said, 'you really don't need to be doing this. As you can see I am fighting fit.'

'Give me a star jump.'

'What?'

'Star jump, jumping jack – whatever you want to call it.'

I considered it, then decided that might be pushing my luck. 'OK, maybe not that fighting fit yet,' I conceded. 'I'm getting there though.'

'See, you still need me after all.' He smiled. 'Maybe once the quiche is in the oven, I can try a light massage, Susan said that might help once you were doing a bit better. If you're OK with that?'

'Yeah that'd be good.' Wow, that was my best performance yet – inside I was screaming but outside I played it proper cool. I wanted to suggest I had some other body parts that would benefit from his attentions... Maybe another time. No! I have to maintain the assumption he's straight until he gives me a rock-solid reason to think otherwise. I don't want him going all 'no homo' on me and breaking this illusion I've created.

We talked while Gabriel prepared the quiche. General getting to know each other stuff, and also what we'd been up to since Monday morning. We talked about his studies and his family. Then I dropped into the conversation that I'd called bingo at my nana's retirement village last night – just to see how he'd react. Turns out he was intrigued, asking question after question. I'd never given it much thought – it was just something I did, a regular part of my week. It was nice to talk about Nana and her friends without being mocked mercilessly for 'hanging out with the old biddies'.

'All right, it's in,' Gabriel said, closing the oven door and turning around and clapping his hands together.

'Massage time, get down on your front and I'll get to work.'

If only… Did this guy even hear himself?

I did as instructed, pushing the coffee table aside – while holding my core, important – then lay down on the rug in the lounge.

I'd considered taking this massage to the bedroom, but that'd be too much like getting my own hopes up. And I still had that pile of junk I'd cleared out of my wardrobe to sort out. So, lounge it was. Keep this G-rated.

I was face down, very conscious of Gabriel approaching, then kneeling down to straddle me. His knees were on the rug either side of me, pinning my arms to my sides. His thighs pressed against my backside. There was so much of him pressed against so much of me – the layers of denim doing little to lessen my awareness.

I hadn't even registered that his hands were already working on my shoulders, pressing with firm, long and slow movements.

'Arthur?'

'Sorry, what? Did you say something?'

'I just asked if it was OK,' Gabriel said, concern in his

voice.

'Oh, fuck yes. I mean, yes. Good.'

He laughed. 'Good, let me know if it hurts, or it's too hard or fast.'

'It's perfect. Just like that, long and slow, feels amazing.' Now it seemed it was my turn to watch what I was saying. Can you blame me? I mean, I have this hunk of man literally on top, pressing into me.

I could feel my body coming to life as he slowly worked his way down my back. A significant part of my anatomy had woken up and was nudging against the floor. This scene had blasted past my intended G-rating and was now nudging at an R-rating.

I sure was glad to be on my front. I could enjoy this massage without dying from embarrassment when my body betrayed me – practically a guarantee by this point.

Gabriel slowly worked his way back up and down once more in silence. I'm glad he wasn't talking – I don't think I was in any state to provide coherent responses.

By the end I felt like a puddle of jelly, but equally a knot of sexual anticipation and frustration. I managed to get out a 'Thank you' as he climbed off me and went to check on the quiche.

I was only just easing myself off the floor when he came back into the lounge.

'You OK? I didn't break you again, did I?'

'No, no,' I said. 'Didn't break me. I feel fantastic. Just took a minute to remember how to function.'

I wasn't about to tell him why I was taking my time getting up.

'My tab is growing by the hour!' I said, clambering onto the couch with real effort. 'Cooked meals, grocery deliveries, back massages… I've got some serious catching up to do.'

'Don't you worry, I'll start calling it in once you can give me a burpee without breaking yourself.'

'Deal.'

Chapter 8
What are you doing here?

Gabriel's quiche was almost as delicious as the man himself, judging by the little I tasted as I inhaled it.

'Anyone would think I'd left you to starve,' Gabriel said. 'Slow down or you'll get indiges— Uh... I sound like my mother.'

Gabriel looked mortified. He doused his portion of quiche with sweet chilli sauce and forked the food in almost as fast as I had. I presume his sudden urgency had more to do with excusing himself from conversation than anything else – it was cute.

We were just finishing up and there were still at least four more decent-sized portions. 'I'll divvy these up for you to take to work, if you like?'

I shook my head in disbelief. 'I'm never going to catch up, am I? Leftovers for lunch now too... You're a keeper!'

Gabriel paused for a moment with his final forkful halfway to his mouth, looked down at his empty plate and finished off his portion. He looked suddenly very self-conscious.

Shit! Why does my mouth say these things, like it's on auto-pilot half the time? I didn't mean it *that way*, it's just a thing you say. But in this situation I suppose I did subconsciously mean it that way too.

I opened my mouth to clarify – read: dig my hole deeper – when the doorbell rang.

The timing of these interruptions – it was uncanny. I couldn't have written it better for myself. I took my opportunity, shooting out of my chair and fleeing the room.

Never will I take vacuum salespeople or hopeful missionaries for granted again.

I opened the front door.

'All right, you gammy old bastard?' Richard said.

'We're glad you're still alive and kicking, mate,' Jared said, clapping me on the shoulder as they came in.

I rescind my recent observation – I think I'd rather suffer the awkward aftermath of my earlier throwaway comment.

Though I will be forever grateful they didn't come in during the massage. Firstly, it would've meant my time under Gabriel's expert hands was cut short. But more importantly, Richard would've had a field day, and I didn't want Gabriel getting embarrassed for his excellent work.

'What have you been doing in here, it smells amazing?' Jared said.

'Yeah, you can't cook. Is your mother here to check on her baby?' Richard said. Then before I could answer he cooed, 'Denise!'

There was no stopping them as they bustled into the kitchen.

'It's Nurse Gabriel!' Richard said. 'What are you doing here?'

'He stopped in to check on me, between classes and his

shift at the driving range,' I said in a feeble attempt to take control of this situation.

'Where's Denise?' Richard said. He had a one track mind, and unfortunately that track often focussed on his affection for my mother.

'She's not here,' I said, growing impatient.

'Who made this then?' Jared said, picking up the hot quiche dish then immediately dropping it again.

'Gabriel did.'

'What? He cooks? A man of many talents,' Jared said, nodding with approval.

Gabriel smiled.

'Smells fantastic anyway!' Richard said, not caring how the quiche came into being, just that it was there. 'Looks like you've got plenty too... Arthur, grab us a plate, will you? I want to see if it tastes as good as it smells.'

There was no coming between Richard and his stomach, so I grabbed a plate for him, Jared too. They pulled up a chair and shovelled the remainder of the quiche – what I had estimated to be four portions – onto their plates. So much for enjoying leftovers for lunch.

And what had happened to Jared's gym-approved meal regime? Looks like he'd fallen off the wagon again – not that he really needed to be so strict about it.

While they had their mouths full I took the chance to ask, 'What are you guys doing here, anyway?'

'Come to check up on you, of course,' Richard said as if wounded.

'Very thoughtful, but shouldn't you be at work?'

'I got back from my out-of-town job early,' Jared said, 'so I swung by to grab Richard on my way here. You know, make sure you hadn't knocked yourself out in the bathtub.'

'But there was no need. Old mate Gabriel here has been looking after you proper,' Richard said. 'Fattening you up with cooked lunches too by the looks. This is delicious,' he said, turning to Gabriel.

'You could've just messaged,' I offered.

'But we haven't seen our darling Arthur in days, have we Jared?' Richard said.

'Nope, and we wanted to see how you were going, you know, physically.'

'Yes! And now we arrive at the crux of this check-up,' Richard said, resting his elbows on the table and knitting his fingers together as he leaned forward. 'Nurse Gabriel—'

'Not a nurse,' Gabriel said, cutting him off.

'—in your expert opinion—'

'Not an expert.'

Richard continued unperturbed, '—how would you describe Arthur's current condition?'

'He's doing well,' Gabriel said, 'watching how he's been holding himself today' – he's been watching me? – 'and based on how well he coped with the massage—'

'Massage?' Richard said, shooting upright and glaring at me. 'When was this? Did you get a massage without me? Was it... strictly business? Or happy ending?'

I dropped my face into my hands.

Seeing that I was no use, Gabriel answered, 'I gave him the massage.'

Jared and Richard stared in stunned silence.

'You... gave him a massage?' Richard said.

'Well, there was nothing untoward about it. And I did buy him lunch first, so...'

Richard broke out in a hearty laugh.

Jared joined in, 'Arthur, I like this guy.'

'He's a keeper all right,' Richard said, unknowingly echoing my earlier comment.

I didn't have time to get awkward about that before Jared piped up again, 'Gabriel, what are you up to on Friday night?'

'No need to answer that, Gabriel,' I said. 'Jared, don't be so nosy.'

'No grand plans, I don't think – how come?'

'It's Artie-fart's big birthday!' Richard said. 'And we have big plans. With the birthday boy feeling fit – we can't have him flying at half-mast, if you know what I mean – we're full steam ahead.'

'Yeah, do you want to join us?' Jared said.

'You don't have to answer that either,' I said. 'Don't feel obligated to come, you've already done more than enough for me.'

'I wouldn't want to impose. We've only just met each other – it would be weird, right?' Gabriel said.

'You've been giving our boy massages and cooking him quiche, we flew past weird ages ago,' Richard said.

'How about this: I'm inviting you,' Jared said. 'You can be my plus-one for Arthur's birthday.'

'Done deal!' Richard said, slamming the table like the matter was settled.

How did I end up in these situations? Strong-armed into doing whatever my friends wanted. I mean, I wanted to see more of Gabriel and this was an easy excuse. But I just knew whatever Richard and Jared had planned would be an absolute clusterfuck of cringe. I almost broke out in a sweat just thinking about how self-conscious I'd be.

'I'd love to come, if Arthur is happy to have me,' Gabriel said.

'Hear that? He'd *love* to come,' Jared said. 'What's more to say?'

There was no way to stop this now, not without making Gabriel think he was unwelcome – and I didn't want that.

'I'd be happy to have you there,' I said. I was pleased, excited, anxious and terrified all at once.

'It's a date!' Richard said. 'Oh it will be a night to remember. With the three of us wingmanning, our main man Arthur is finally gonna get some, I can feel it.' Then he turned to Gabriel and put on his serious face. 'But we haven't told the birthday boy what's happening on Friday, and we don't yet know where your allegiances lie, so you can't be trusted with the truth either – not yet.'

'It's for his own good,' Jared said, 'in case he gets it into his head to sabotage the night. He's done it before – called ahead and cancelled the granny lap dance – can you believe that?'

'No, I can't,' Gabriel said, smiling. 'Why would you do such a thing, Arthur?'

I groaned – here I was hoping I'd recruit Gabriel onto Team Arthur. But it looked like I'd already lost. Maybe it was for the best? The night would be a train wreck, Gabriel would see how much of a pack of losers we were and he'd be gone before we'd even finished our first pint.

'Friday night it is,' Richard said, clapping me on the back, 'Arthur's big day.'

'Time to break the drought,' Jared said.

'Dust off the sheets.'

'Take a trip to pound town.'

'Yes, got it, thanks guys,' I said.

'Go for a bit of the old in-and-out.'

'A round of "hide the sausage".'

'Hot beef injection.'

'Collaborative nap time.'

'Bump uglies.'

'Foxtrot Uniform Charlie Kilo.'

My head was back in my hands by this point. There would be no stopping them now…

After a while I looked up, catching Gabriel's eye as Richard and Jared egged each other on. He gave me a brief smile – in solidarity? Sympathy? Mocking? I managed a feeble smile in return. What was I getting myself into?

Chapter 9
What's got your knickers in a twist?

Today was the day. My 'big day' as Richard insisted on calling it.

I was back at work yesterday. Physically present – and able – but mentally I was a million miles away. My mind had alternated between daydreaming about Gabriel and working myself up to coming out to Richard and Jared.

I'd decided I'd had enough pissing around. Enough false starts. Enough half-hearted attempts. Today, I was coming out. It was my birthday, and I'd ruin it if I wanted to.

It's not like I'm getting any less gay, so my friends needed to know at some point. Potential bonus: they might get off my back about finding a girl? A guy can dream.

And if Gabriel's weird about me coming out, that's fine too. I might as well establish where we stand now. No point in us both wasting time building up a friendship only to drop it when my surprise gayness made things uncomfortable.

Jared and Richard had skived off work again, headed home early to change, and met at my place for a drink. They took this opportunity to drop tidbits about their plans for our evening. It sounded like they were just going to get me trolleyed and try to foist me on some poor, unsuspecting girl. So, the usual – I could manage that.

I was feeling somewhat more at ease now as we headed down to the pub. At least I didn't have to worry about my friends making more of a fool of me than usual.

I only had to worry about opening up about my longest and most closely held secret.

**

'How about her?' Jared said, pointing out a Sporty Spice look-alike across the pub. 'I know how you prefer the athletic ones, more natural-looking make-up, less dressy, all that.'

'Nice buns too, perfect for our Arthur, a butt man through and through,' Richard said. 'We know I'm a tits man myself.'

That we did, his previous girlfriends were a string of busty women – though each lasted only a month or two. Lucy was no exception when it came to cup size, but they'd been together for almost two years now and were still going strong. None of us, Richard included, could fathom what she saw in him, but we weren't questioning a good thing.

'Go on, buddy,' Jared said. 'Go get yourself a piece of that.'

'No need to be so vulgar,' I said. 'Come on guys, have some class.'

'Oh! Come now, your majesty.' Richard said.

'You do seem snappy, even more highly strung than you were at the driving range last weekend,' Jared said. 'And we all know how that ended up.'

It was true. I was a great big knot of nerves, worse than Sunday by far.

'Yeah, what's got your knickers in a twist? Out with it!' Richard said. 'We can't have you distracted, not tonight of all nights.'

I had to tell them. This wasn't going to get any easier. I'd already used getting a fresh round and a trip to the bathroom to escape the conversation when it was charting into dangerous waters tonight.

'Guys, you've known me for a long time, right? Since we started school in Miss Bedford's class,' I said, easing myself into it.

'Yes we know, Arthur,' Jared said, 'we were there.'

'Yes, yes you were,' I said. 'That's how we met, became friends and have been ever since. We've been through a lot of change since then. Some good, some bad, some neither. Jared, your parents split, and you were not in a good way for a long time. But then you scored that big scholarship, and recently your promotion. Richard, your grandparents who practically raised you, both dying less than a year apart from each other—'

'OK mate, how much longer are you going to go on telling us things we already know?' Jared said.

'Not our fondest memories either – this is meant to be a celebration!' Richard said.

'I only wanted to say that we've been through a lot of change, and no doubt we'll go through even more. But I never want those changes to destroy our friendship—'

'Arthur... Did you forget to take your pills or

something?' Jared said. 'You're all over the show.'

'And so soppy.'

'What I've been trying to say is—'

'Gabriel!' Richard shouted over my shoulder. 'Backup has arrived.'

'Here to save us from this doom and gloom,' Jared said.

'You take a seat, cheer Arthur up for us,' Richard said. 'It's my round, back in a sec.'

Gabriel slid into the booth next to me. 'What's the deal?'

'Arthur's having a premature mid-life crisis – a one-third life crisis?' Jared said. 'That's what you get for spending all that time with the oldies.'

I laughed, not from anything funny he'd said. More from the unexpected relief of not having to follow through with coming out, not yet anyway. 'I just need a drink.'

'That's more like it,' Jared said, beaming. 'And here's the barmaid herself!'

Richard dropped four pints and a table number in front of us. 'The finest mudwater gentlemen.'

'The nectar of the gods!' Jared said – he was on fine form tonight.

Gabriel picked up his pint and turned to face me. 'Happy birthday Arthur,' he said, smiling and clinking his glass against mine.

I melted.

I took a swig from my pint to prevent myself doing or saying anything embarrassing. Unfortunately I was so busy acting normal that my body forgot to swallow. I ended up choking on my beer, coughing and spluttering for a good ten seconds before regaining control of my breathing.

'Told you, the boy's not right,' Jared said. 'Gabriel, I think you broke our Arthur.'

'You didn't! Don't worry,' I said, 'I'm fine. Just went in the wrong hole.'

'That's what she said.' Richard and Jared high-fived.

'You're better than that, Rich,' I said.

'No he's not! Have you even met him?' Jared said, laughing along with Richard.

A waitress approached our table. 'I've got the triple cooked chips, crispy squid and mozzarella sticks.'

'Chuck 'em all down there sweetheart,' Richard said.

She frowned at the endearment. 'The rest will be out shortly.'

'The rest? How much did you order?' Jared said.

'My dear friends, we have too much drinking to get done to stop for dinner, so I ordered everything on the Sides menu.'

'Everything?' Jared said, eyes wide with delight.

'Indeed. Along with these three dishes, coming our way we have onion rings, chargrilled sweetcorn, buffalo wings, nachos and Scotch eggs. Two portions of each, to be sure we have enough.'

We barely had room to put down our pints once all the food was on the table. It was a decidedly beige affair – smelt amazing though.

'So much deep-fried deliciousness,' Jared said, formerly so strict with his gym-approved diet. Friday was his designated cheat day, and he always went all out. Not that he'd been holding back on any other day of late.

'Amazing, right? The sweetcorn isn't deep-fried though. Being the responsible adult that I am, I knew we still needed to get in one of our five a day, even on Artie-fart's birthday.'

The conversation took a break while we sampled each of the dishes.

'Oof. Artie, maybe take a pass on the buffalo wings,' Richard said. 'Can't have you gassing some poor girl while she's going to town down there.'

'Why are you singling me out for that advice?' I said, feeling emboldened by the booze.

'Because you don't have a steel-lined stomach like I do,' Richard said, patting his ample belly. 'And Jared here – our resident heartbreaker – is taking one for the team. He's suspending his own hunt for the evening to focus all his efforts and talents on tracking your prey.'

'Sounds like a nature doco,' Gabriel said. 'You fancy yourself a young David Attenborough, do you Richard?'

'Too right I do,' Richard said, before clearing his throat and putting on his best, deep narrator's voice. 'A young, male homosapien visits his local watering hole. Here he feasts and quenches his mighty thirst amongst fellow members of his pack. He is in his prime, and tonight he hunts for a mate.'

I couldn't help but laugh – Richard's gravelly voice was made to narrate.

'And I – the pack's alpha male, obviously – will devour all the buffalo wings I like,' Jared said, gnawing on his fourth. 'And fart to my heart's content' – gross – 'because at the end of the evening I'll be going home with Arthur's usual date.'

'The Right Honourable Lady Palmer,' Richard said, high-fiving Jared with a greasy hand.

'You guys need new material,' I said. I suspect they considered the gag was ripe for recycling with their new audience member.

'And you, my dear friend, need to find yourself a date,' Jared said. 'That busybody neighbour of yours – what was her name again?'

'He's not that desperate yet, mate,' Richard said.

'Nah, nah, nah. Just, what's her name?' Jared said.

'Patty,' I said.

'Yes! That nosy witch has practically been throwing her niece at you for years. You need to at least take her for a ride, break her poor wee heart, then she'll never speak to you again. And neither will Patty, if you're lucky – double win!'

'You know there's no way I'd do that,' I said. 'I'm not as ruthless or heartless as you, Jared.'

'Too nice! That's what you are,' Jared said as he jumped up to get a fresh round.

'Indeed,' Richard said, 'a big old softy.' He licked the last of the greasy bar snacks from his fingers. They had demolished everything in front of them. Slowly sinking back into the spill-proof upholstery they sipped their beers, sighing in contentment.

'I think what I need after all that is a lie down,' I said after a while.

'You'll be doing no such thing, my boy! Not alone, anyway,' Jared said with a wink as he returned, plonking the fresh handles down.

What round were we on now? Six, seven? I'd lost count.

'Yes, back to business,' Richard said. 'I have a little exercise for us, a thought experiment if you will. Arthur, my friend, you're a nice guy, good looking too. If I was into dudes, I would totally bang you. Right, Gabey-baby? What do you think? Maybe I'm biased, been mates with this bastard too long. He's a good bloke, easy on the eye too, isn't he?'

I couldn't be dealing with this right now. I took a swig as

he talked, downing half of my fresh pint in one go – hiding from the embarrassment.

You cannot ask someone that. Especially not in front of the person you're talking about. And not just any old someone, the someone I hadn't been able to get off my mind since meeting him – which wasn't even a week ago but felt like forever.

Richard didn't give him a chance to respond – or myself time to bluster an interruption – before launching across the table and grabbing me on either side. 'Look at these *masculine* shoulders. Ladies love that! And these *shapely* pecs,' he continued, pawing at my front despite my protests. 'I can appreciate a nice chest, even on a bloke. Mind you, Arthur's isn't as nice as Gabe's there, but still, nothing to sniff at. And this face' – he pinched my cheeks, like you see old ladies do to small children – 'is adorable! I have it on good authority that lady bits are regularly set a-quiver in the vicinity of this visage,' Richard said. He dropped back onto his side of the table, arms out towards me. 'All round, he's a catch.'

'A-grade man meat,' Jared said. 'Girls would die to get a piece of that.'

'I rest my case, your honour,' Richard said.

'You know,' Gabriel said after a pause, looking thoughtful, 'I think you're right. I mean, I certainly wouldn't kick him out of bed.'

'See!' Richard shouted, triumphant. 'Even this hunk wants a piece of our birthday boy.'

'Are you sure it's not you boys that want a piece of him?' Gabriel said. 'You've just sold me on his desirable attributes – of which there are many.'

'Ew, no,' Jared said.

'Arthur's like a brother,' Richard said.

'Practically incestuous.'

'Plus he's got hairy legs.'

'Can't be rubbing up against that in bed.'

'Nope, can't be done.'

'Now you're trying to backtrack?' Gabriel said.

'No, not backtracking – clarifying why he's not the one for us,' Richard said.

Gabriel looked thoughtful, then smiled. 'All right then boys, I'm sold. I'll take him off your hands.'

Jared laughed. 'Even with his dicky back?'

'I'll take all of him, just as he is.'

I slammed down the empty pint I'd guzzled during the back and forth between these three. They'd barely started on their fresh pints.

Even half-cut, there was only so much ribbing I could take. Not when it was cutting so close to the bone – I couldn't laugh this off like I usually would.

'I'll grab a fresh round,' I said, clambering past Gabriel to escape the booth. This earnt me funny looks from both Richard and Jared, but I didn't catch Gabriel's reaction – I was too busy avoiding eye contact.

Their stares were boring into my back though. I could feel them as I slunk to the bar.

I was suddenly very conscious of my walking – why did it feel so unnatural?

By the time I reached the bar I was shaking. Gripping it for support, I was glad when the bartender asked if I was after another round, requiring only a nod from me.

I needed to calm down.

It wasn't their fault, they didn't realise the turmoil they were causing – how could they? I hadn't told them.

I was being melodramatic. Such a diva.
But what was I going to do?

Chapter 10
What was he saying?

My breathing had almost returned to normal, and the bartender was still pulling the pints when I sensed someone beside me.

'Sorry if I got carried away,' Gabriel said, 'I—'

'No, you shouldn't be the one apologising,' I said, trying to smile. 'I was the one who scarpered. I... I'm not used to being the centre of attention. Or getting so many compliments.'

'Well, I'm sorry for upsetting you anyway... But I meant every word I said before.' Gabriel smiled, grabbed the two nearest pints and turned to take them back to the table.

He left me at the bar trying to recall what exactly he'd said before.

I'd paid for the beers and returned to the table on auto-pilot, sliding into the booth beside Gabriel.

What had he said? What was he saying? Was he gay? Was he hitting on me? Or is that my wishful thinking? Maybe he was trying to pump me up, complimenting me in a generic, platonic kind of way. Had to be, right?

I was still processing what he'd said when I tuned back into the conversation.

'—it's your birthday!' Richard said. 'As we were saying before you so rudely abandoned us... If you stopped being such a sorry case for a second you could pull any bit of tail in here. The night's not getting any younger, my boy... What about her?' Richard pointed – not subtle in the slightest – to a brunette with breasts almost bursting from her form-fitting dress. Girl was ready for a big night.

'She's uh... She's more your type, Richard,' I said.

'Aye, that she is,' he conceded.

'What about the blonde on the corner of the bar?' Jared said, talking louder now that the music had been turned up.

'What, the one with the boyfriend?'

'Pfft, you could take him.'

'I will not start a bar fight.'

'Spoilsport,' Jared said.

'How cool would that be, though?' Richard said, eyes alight.

'Not a chance,' I said. 'I'm here for a few drinks with my mates on my birthday, that's all.'

'Boring. We might as well go play bingo and die,' Jared said.

'That's it!' Richard said with an air of triumph. 'That's it, Jared. We've been going about this all wrong. He's not interested in any of the girls here... Because our boy prefers more mature women!'

'He's after a cougar,' Jared said.

'That's why he's not giving these lovely ladies a second look. That's why he sees those old biddies at bingo every week.' Richard said, getting excited now. 'Our boy Arthur – kinky bastard – wants himself an older lady.'

'Oh for fuck's sake, I'm gay!'

Conversation in the bar halted.

Had I said that out loud? Shouted it even?

I looked across the table at Richard and Jared who were both staring back at me open-mouthed. Then I shot a shifty glance at Gabriel sitting next to me – he looked equally shocked.

The chatter in the bar had resumed before anyone at the table said anything.

'You're gay,' Richard said. He was glaring at me, brow creased.

'Since when?' Jared said.

Gabriel took a swig from his beer.

I pushed back into the booth seat a little and gritted my teeth. 'Since always.'

'And all these girls we've tried to set—'

'Not interested.'

'But how can you know?' Jared said.

'How do you know that you're straight?' I countered.

'Well,' Jared said, more confused than anything, 'I just know.'

'Exactly,' I said. 'So do I. It just... took me a while to realise.'

'Why didn't you bloody well tell us?' Richard said.

'I uh... I kept it to myself while I was figuring out what was going on.'

'I take it you've figured it out now, seeing as you're telling us?' Richard said.

'Yeah... But I'd been keeping it to myself for so long it was suddenly too daunting to bring it up with anyone else,' I said. 'The longer I left it, the more daunting it became... I was scared.'

'Mate!' Jared said. 'All this time, wasted.'

'Have we been cock blocking you all along?' Richard said, disgusted with himself.

'This changes things Rich,' Jared said. 'Changes them big time. We've got to recalibrate.'

'Jared, indeed we do. If we're going hunting, we need to switch our stun guns to *cock mode*,' Richard said. 'We've got to find our boy a man!'

'He doesn't want himself a grey lady, he's got himself a hunger for some old codger.'

'No! You guys made that up,' I said.

'What? So no old guys either?' Jared said.

'No! Just… guys my age,' I said. 'Or thereabouts.'

'Right, right. So, top or bottom?' Richard said.

'Wh— what?' Where was he getting his information?

'Yeah, do you prefer to be the uh… the pounder, or the poundee?' added Jared unhelpfully.

'I am *not* telling you that,' I said.

'Both then,' Jared said.

'Greedy bastard,' Richard said.

'Why not though, right?' Jared said. 'Get it any way you can.'

'Got to be one of the perks. The gays love it, must be good or they wouldn't do it,' Richard said. Then he turned to Gabriel, who – since I'd burst out with my announcement – had been alternating between great chugs of beer and sitting in stunned silence. 'So, Gabes. Did you know our boy liked the cock?'

I'd just taken a sip, but at that comment choked it back up again.

'Uh… No, no I didn't,' Gabriel said. He looked down into his empty pint then back up at me. 'But I'd hoped so.'

He what?

'Nurse Gabriel!' Jared screamed.

'He wants a bit of our Arthur!' Richard said, bouncing up and down on his seat.

'Get in there, son.'

'Mission accomplished.'

'I—' I didn't know what to say.

I looked to Gabriel. The blood had rushed to his face while he stared into the depths of his pint glass.

'Is that true?' I said.

After what felt like forever, Gabriel looked up at me. 'Yeah… Since you ran into me, actually.'

'Not my finest moment,' I said.

'My hands may have lingered longer than strictly necessary in holding you up.'

'Copping a feel, the dirty bugger,' Jared said, grinning with approval.

'I was in the office afterwards trying to manufacture another interaction. That's when you caned yourself at the tee,' Gabriel said.

'That he did,' Jared said.

'Not quite what I had in mind,' Gabriel said, 'and it pained me to see you in such agony, but it gave me a solid excuse to see you again.'

'This scoundrel had designs on our Arthur from the get go!' Richard said, shaking his head in amusement. I watched as he downed his pint which had been near full only moments ago. 'Oh! Would you look at that – tide's out. Time for the next round,' he said getting up. 'Jared, give me a hand, will you?'

'What? Bloody get them yourself, you don't need me holding your—'

Richard was jerking his head to the side, eyes bugged out. It was not subtle, but then nothing Richard did was subtle. And Jared wouldn't have registered otherwise.

'Oh… Right!' Jared said. 'Oof, look at that – quite the crowd at the bar, might take us a while.'

'Back in a bit,' Richard said, winking like a filthy, drunken pervert.

Silence descended at the table again.

'So…'

'So, you're gay too?' I dared to ask. It seemed redundant, but I had to be sure.

'Yeah,' he said. 'And I… There's no way to say this without sounding cheesy, but I think you're something special.'

It was cheesy, but coming from Gabriel it didn't sound so ridiculous, and I wanted to believe it. 'You should have said something.'

'I did! I've been dropping hints, almost constantly actually. Couldn't come right out with it, could I? In case you were straight, or plain not interested. And I didn't want to make you uncomfortable in your own place.'

'I'd convinced myself that you were just a really nice guy,' I said. 'Didn't dare get my hopes up.'

'I dared,' he said. 'And it's been infuriating. You never took the bait when I made a move but you never rejected me outright either. I couldn't gauge what you were thinking or feeling.'

I couldn't think how to explain that I hadn't stopped thinking about him either, not since I'd run into him. Even in my dreams. How the sight of him lifted my spirits and got my heart pumping. How I was getting anxious that he'd have no reason to come around any more once I'd recovered.

There was no way to explain, so instead I leant in and kissed him.

I was beginning to think I'd made a terrible miscalculation when he started kissing me back.

My skin was tingling as his hand came up behind my head, fingers in my hair. I felt his lips press into mine, the warmth of his touch. It felt like he was enveloping me. We were in our own little world, and everything else faded from my mind.

Then there was a howl, wrenching me from my cocoon of warm fuzzies.

Richard was still going when he bounced back to the table with Jared, both of them grinning like hyenas as they sat down across from us. With the illusion shattered the thump of music broke into my consciousness. And these people – where had they all come from?

'That didn't take long,' Richard said, delighted. 'I didn't catch it, who made the first move?'

Gabriel smiled. 'Arthur did, he wanted to shut me up.'

'I did not! I just… I didn't know what… I didn't want to waste any more time.'

'That's my boy,' Jared said.

'And to think,' Richard said, 'none of this would've happened if our Arthur hadn't been wound so tight at the driving range.'

'Nurse Gabriel would never have charmed Arthur's number out of him, and ministered to his needs,' Jared said.

'Speaking of, Arthur mentioned he was feeling a little niggle in his back,' Gabriel said.

'What?' I said. 'No, my back is feeling—'

'It might benefit from another massage, later tonight,'

Gabriel said.

'Oh… Oh! Yes, ouch. Very sore,' I said, finally realising what was being said. If I thought my heart was pumping before, now it was leaping from my chest. 'Should sort that out, sooner rather than later.'

'Let's get you home,' Gabriel said. 'I'll take care of it, if that's OK with you?'

'Yes, very OK. It needs your attention,' I said.

I was shameless. Blame the booze.

'Don't you boys worry about us,' Jared said, waving his hand at us. 'We achieved everything we set out to do tonight.'

'Just make sure you don't break our Arthur's gay little heart,' Richard said. 'Won't you?'

'I would never,' Gabriel said, his playful smile replaced with a look of stern resolution. It was adorable.

'Enough of that,' I said. 'I've got other organs I'm focused on right now.'

Richard beamed. 'Go forth and fornicate, my son.'

Who was I to argue with that? This was the best birthday ever, and it had barely even begun.

I left the bar with a smile on my face and Gabriel's hand in my own.

Thank you for reading

I hope you enjoyed the story. If you did, please tell your friends – personal recommendations are the best! Also please consider leaving reviews on Amazon and Goodreads. This is important in making my work more visible to other readers – each review gives the books a little boost in the charts, meaning others are more likely to stumble across them.

For my latest updates and a free short story you can join the mailing list on my website: www.gbralph.com. You can also find my other stories there, and links to my social media if you'd like to drop me a message – I'd love to hear from you!

But before you go…

The story continues...

Slip and Slide
Rise and Shine – Book Two

A gay romantic comedy novella about wading through the noise to discover what you really want.

Caught in the crossfire of his chaotic flatmates' one-sided romance, and a landlady on a rampage, Gabriel is just trying to get to work on time and avoid burning dinner.

Throw in a plumbing emergency, overstaying cats, a public and painful proclamation of love, and a trip to the hospital – even the laid-back Gabriel is frazzling.

Then there's Arthur. Sweet, adorable, and eager to please – all qualities that had so charmed Gabriel. Though, that's also how you might describe a puppy. And puppies are a lot of work.

Gabriel has his man –
now he must decide if Arthur is worth it...

Slip and Slide is the sequel to Duck and Dive, but this time Gabriel's calling the shots.

Want to dive right in?

Grab yourself a copy of *Slip and Slide*:
www.gbralph.com/slip-and-slide

Or, read a sneak preview right now...

Chapter 1
We love him though, don't we?

'Come on, Theo! What are you doing in there?' I said, knocking on the bathroom door.

'I am *trying* to have a nice, relaxing bath,' he said through the door. 'And your banging is devastating to my chill, so beat it.'

Claire wandered past, taking a bite from her toast. 'What's the bet that skinny, white boy is beating something else in there,' she said, winking as she headed from the kitchen into the living room. 'He'll be luxuriating in a nice, long wan—'

'Yes, got it. Ew,' I said. 'But... you're probably right.'

'I'm right, Gabriel,' Claire said as she stepped over the neighbour's cat – Betty – and skirted around the easel and half-formed sculptures. The moment she dropped onto the couch, Betty hopped up next to her.

'First: why must he do it in our *shared* bathroom? And second: why *right now*? I've got my shift this morning,' I said, then turned to cast my voice through the closed door, 'like I do *every week*.'

'You know our Theo – our resident whirlwind of obliviousness – do you really think he's aware what day it is?' Claire said, idly patting the cat. After sipping her tea, she cleared her throat and raised her voice. 'Theo. Stop jerking off and let Gramps in, he's got work.'

The reaction was immediate. 'Sorry, Claire! I'll be out in a minute,' he said, coupled with sounds of water sloshing about and things crashing to the floor.

'Why does he listen to you?'

'He may be too wrapped up in his own world to consider most anyone else... but he's infatuated with me,' she said, 'obviously.'

'What? No, he's not.' I turned from the bathroom to focus on Claire, serene as ever, eating her breakfast under Betty's watchful eye. We never fed the cats, only put out water for them, but they were ever hopeful.

I noticed Basil then too, the neighbour's other cat. The lump of ginger fur napping in his usual corner spot, high on the couch back. From his perch, Basil could survey the room – like a king on his throne, deigning to grant his subjects an audience with their monarch. Provided the peasants remained at arm's length with no undignified touching.

'Look at Theo's paintings and sculptures,' Claire said, gesturing to the numerous pieces of art scattered around our living room. The works were at varying stages of incompleteness, the product of frantic and feverish all-nighters. Jugs of instant coffee, microwave pizza, and pot noodles sustained his efforts, inevitably followed by two days crashed on his bed.

'So,' she said, 'do you notice anything?'

'They're all half-baked and making a mess of our living room?' The only time I ever looked was when I needed to shuffle something aside to clear a path, or adjust a drop-cloth to catch any paint splotches. 'I've never considered Theo's art, not properly.'

'Well, not really your favoured subject matter, is it?' Claire said.

I looked now, really looked. 'There *are* a lot of breasts, aren't there?'

'Yes, well, he is a rather sexually repressed straight boy, so...'

'And his subjects, they all have dark skin. Dark, curly hair...' I looked to Claire, to Theo's art, then back to my flatmate again. 'They're all *you*.'

Claire clapped, though it was more sarcastic than triumphant.

I scowled. 'I hadn't noticed.'

'Age really doesn't equal wisdom, does it?'

'Hey, I'm only a few years older than you two.'

'More like six or seven years, old man.'

Unlike Theo, Claire was smart, focused, organised. A science student, majoring in geology – a solid degree. And mature beyond her years, Claire was unnervingly perceptive. Without me saying a word, she knew I was struggling in this new city, away from everyone and everything I knew.

Theo burst from the bathroom then, towel wrapped around his skinny waist, and wet hair covering half of his face like a raggedy old mop. At least he'd washed it for once. 'Sorry, Claire. Didn't realise you were up already.'

'Free cardio class at the Rec Centre this morning, isn't it?' Claire said. She too had a lot of hair, but it always looked good – Claire made everything look effortless.

'Oh, yeah. Right, of course,' Theo said, still standing in the doorway in his towel. Was he… was he posing? Claire was so right.

'What am I, chopped liver?' I said, still waiting for the bathroom.

'Uh? What *are* you talking about?' Theo said, turning to face me with his habitual look of incomprehension.

'Never mind, get out,' I said, shooing him away.

'All right, Gramps,' Theo said, relaxing his pose and stepping aside. These two really made me feel like a grumpy old prick sometimes.

I'd finally made it into the bathroom and slammed the door behind me. It'd have to be a quick turnaround if I wasn't going to be late. In my haste to get the shower going, I slipped on the puddles of water Theo had left. I grabbed a hold of the tap, saving myself from crashing to the floor.

I took a breath, pulled myself to vertical and turned on the shower. There was a wobble in the tap I'm sure wasn't there before, but it was working fine now – I'd have to keep an eye on it.

I shed my clothes and stepped under the stream of hot water over the bath tub.

They were all right, really – my flatmates. It was good to have people around when I got home.

Having worked straight out of school and now starting university at 26 years old, I was considered a 'mature student'. Surrounded by teens and early twenty-somethings every day, I was an oddity, a curiosity, but one that most seemed unwilling to investigate too closely. I'd had trouble meeting people my own age because they were all working, living their adult lives, like I should be. I was stuck in some kind of social limbo. To be fair, I had met some people, but the friendships didn't extend beyond class. And I'd even met a guy – that went well... until it didn't. But we don't talk about that.

Anyway... Claire, Theo and I were an odd trio, but we'd met at the flat viewing and seemed willing to take a punt on each other and the flat. We signed up on the spot. The cheap rent was the clincher – it meant I only had to pick up a few shifts at the driving range each week. And working there doubled as an opportunity to meet people too – I was ever hopeful.

I finished my shower and changed into my uniform. This was cutting it fine, but I still ought to make it to work on time. I threw my book, drink bottle and lunch into my backpack, and headed for the front door.

I almost had it open when I caught a whiff of the mat.

'Fuck's sake, Basil!'

'What? What's happened?' Claire said, stalking out of her bedroom. 'He's asleep on his perch.'

'Pissed on the door mat again, hasn't he?' I said.

'Sneaky little bastard,' Claire said.

I considered leaving it to the others to sort out, but decided against it. Picking up the soiled mat by the corners, I carried it through the flat – trying to avoid inhaling the acrid stench – dropped it into the bathtub and rinsed it off.

'When you gotta go, you gotta go,' Theo said.

I turned to see my flatmate nodding sagely from the bathroom doorway, wearing the same Pikachu top as yesterday. 'Theo... did you change back into the same clothes?'

'Yeah, I didn't spill anything on myself all day yesterday,' Theo said, pulling the hem of his top to show me, looking rather proud of himself. 'So, he's good for another round.'

'You – No. No, I don't have time,' I said, deciding it wasn't worth it.

'Basil is getting on, you know…' Claire said, joining Theo outside the bathroom to watch me wash the mat. 'At least he did it on the mat, right?'

I sighed. 'Yeah. But we'd better watch him when he's in the house.' It was the third time he'd done it this month, but none of us could bring ourselves to lock the little piss-bag out – he was too adorable.

I turned off the water and hung the mat over the towel rail to dry.

'Gabriel, are you off soon?' Claire said.

'Yeah, now. Why?'

'Can you take the rubbish out?'

'I've really got to go, Claire,' I said, trying to get past my flatmates loitering in the doorway.

'It'll only take a sec. It's ready to go – I've tied up the bag in the kitchen.'

'Sure. Yes, OK.' It would be quicker to just do it. I dashed into the kitchen, grabbed the black bag and—

Exposed a pool of sticky liquid on the floor. It reeked almost as bad as the door mat.

'Bin juice!' I investigated the bottom of the black bag to find a neat claw mark with food scraps hanging out, but no cat in sight.

Claire appeared in the kitchen. 'Basil's on form this morning…'

'He's not even our bloody cat.'

'We love him though, don't we? Don't worry Gabriel, I'll clean it up, you go,' she said, waving me out of the flat.

I didn't need any more encouragement so made my escape before I was interrupted again, careful to hold up the bag by the tear to avoid more drippage.

The driving range wasn't far away, but I'd really have to get moving to avoid being late. Not that I'd get my pay docked or anything like that – but my boss, Murray, would *pass comment*. Something passive aggressive about the clock being out because he'd expected me a few minutes ago. Or he'd feign ignorance of the roster, like he didn't know precisely when I should be there. And then I'd have to endure low-key digs all morning about time management and reliability and 'early is on time, on time is late' and yadda yadda yadda. It was not worth it.

The apartment building door swung shut as I dropped the rubbish bag over the railing and stormed down the front steps.

I'd almost made it to the footpath when I heard a shrill call from behind me. 'Mr Bedford!'

My step faltered. I briefly considered pretending I hadn't heard – though, with no headphones on, and the volume and pitch of that screech, no one would believe such a feeble excuse. I'd pay for it later if I didn't turn around.

'Yes, Mrs Sheffield?'

May I introduce our landlady, Sharon Sheffield. She owned and lived in the apartment directly beneath the one we rented from her. We took a perverse pleasure in dropping our rubbish bags on the pile beneath her window – the building's designated drop-off point. With such a sight and smell, Sharon was forced to keep her kitchen windows and blinds closed.

'Ah, young man, I'm glad to have caught you. Are you heading out?' she said, calling from her front patio around from the front steps.

'Yes, Mrs Sheffield, I'm off to work,' I said, trying to edge away.

'You're a good boy, aren't you? So hard-working, and all while studying full time. Polite too, not like the young people in my other properties.'

I took a breath to halt the snide responses on the tip of my tongue. 'Thank you, Mrs Sheffield—'

'Now, you must call me Sharon, young man. I insist,' she said, chuckling to herself. '"Mrs Sheffield" makes me sound so old, I'm no matron yet.'

Who was she kidding?

'Now, that's pronounced Sha-RON, mind you, emphasis on the second syllable. Have I told you about the origins of my name?'

'Actually, yes—'

'It's Hebrew and means "the valley". It's also the name of the rose of Sharon that Jesus plucked on his way to Galilee. "I am the rose of Sharon, the lily of the valley." That's from the King James translation of the Song of Solomon. Isn't it wonderful?'

'Indeed it is, Sharon. But I really must get to—'

'Yes, yes, of course. I was just calling out because I wanted to remind you about the Residents Committee meeting this week. As Chairperson I highly encourage attendance by all residents – both property owners like me and tenants such as yourself – we haven't had representation from you or the other two for months now.'

Our landlady took on the role of Residents Committee Chairperson a few years ago, having run unopposed. And so, emboldened by her victory, the first item on her agenda was relocating the rubbish pile.

'Mm, yes, we've all been very busy,' I said, attempting to edge away again.

'Of course, of course. But the rubbish issue – front of mind for many residents – is on the agenda again this week. We last discussed it six months ago, and I believe it's time to reconsider, especially with the warmer weather strengthening the uh… the aroma. It would be a real help to have your support at the meeting.'

That mound of stinking black bags wouldn't be going anywhere – not when it was already so convenient for everyone else, and more importantly, not outside their windows.

I gave no response, so she continued, 'It's on Wednesday evening, 7pm.'

'Oh, that's unfortunate,' I said, a blatant lie. 'I have the evening shift at the driving range on Wednesday so won't be able to attend.' That was true. 'I'll send Theo or Claire in my stead.' Another lie, there was zero chance they'd show.

Sharon pursed her lips at the suggestion. 'Are you sure you won't be available?'

'No, sorry. I've already committed to the shift, can't let my boss down,' I said, playing the responsible young person card, then followed up with the fatal blow. 'And I've got to keep the shifts up, make sure I can keep paying the rent on time.'

'Yes, good boy. Very responsible,' Sharon said, nodding. 'Well, I'd better let you get to work.'

'Have a good day, Mrs – Sharon,' I said, careful to emphasise the second syllable, then turned to go.

'Oh, Mr Bedford. One more thing: have you seen Betty or Basil? They've been going missing more often lately, and they didn't come home at all last night.'

'No idea, sorry. I'm sure they'll turn up soon!' I called back as I turned onto the footpath and out of sight. As much as those fur-bags annoyed us, we wouldn't force the poor creatures back to that woman – we're not monsters.

I powered down the street, risking a glance at the time – I was so late.

Are you keen for more?
Grab yourself a copy of *Slip and Slide*:
www.gbralph.com/slip-and-slide

Acknowledgements

I'd finished the first draft of a novel and put it away to get some distance before coming back to edit later, hopefully with some objectivity. I still wanted to keep up the habit of writing every day and couldn't bring myself to get stuck into another big project right away. So, I thought short stories might be a way to keep it up and clear my head at the same time.

I'd written a few stories based on little ideas I'd squirrelled away on my phone's note app, each only a few pages long. Then I came across this idea I'd noted down: 'Group of friends. One is gay, having trouble coming out to his mates. They unknowingly make it more and more difficult.' I envisioned this as a fun and frustrating scene, just a few pages long like the others. But I was so amused by the characters and ridiculous situations that it grew into a 22,000 word novella. Still, a fun exercise, and that was all I intended for it.

Then the country went into lockdown for Covid-19. My commute had evaporated, as had all evening and weekend plans for the foreseeable future. My partner and I were fortunate to be in good health and able to continue working from home. So, with all this extra time in lockdown, I thought I might as well sort out this story I'd written, tidy it up, edit, format, etc. I learnt independent publishing is fairly involved, but I enjoyed the process.

The Bestseller Experiment podcast, hosted by Mark Stay

and Mark Desvaux, was a valuable resource with useful advice from themselves, bestselling authors, and others in the writing/publishing industry. It's so inspiring and motivational – highly recommended. And their BXP2020 campaign, which encourages people to commit to writing just 200 words a day, was what kicked this story into life.

David Gaughran's *Let's Get Digital: How to Self-Publish, and Why You Should* is packed with practical advice too. It gave me the tools and confidence to take on the big, daunting beast that is publishing, and get my book out there. David discusses how authors aren't just writers, but publishers and marketers too. He makes it clear that writing a good book is up to you, but for the other aspects he explains every step along the way, suggesting where might be best to focus your time, effort and money.

Now, this is the point where I want to thank my partner, Te Peeti, for being brave enough to be the first to read *Duck and Dive*. His reaction now graces the book's description, 'I didn't know what to expect, but I genuinely enjoyed it. I'm glad I did, otherwise that would've been a very awkward conversation.'

I also want to thank him for pushing me to tell people I'd written this. I'd tidied up my story and independently published it on Amazon as a bit of a trial. I just wanted to see how it all worked, with no intentions of taking it any further. Te Peeti told me off and asked what was the point? Surely marketing and promotion should be part of the trial? He was right, of course. Telling people is daunting though, isn't it? Who did I think I was – a geotechnical engineer – writing fiction? Anyway, it's up and I'm telling people now.

And you've read it! So, finally, I want to thank *you* for giving Arthur's story a shot, and I hope you enjoyed it.

Made in United States
Orlando, FL
03 September 2022